THE BIG NAP

"Waldman treats the Los Angeles scene with humor, offers a revealing glimpse of Hasidic life, and provides a surprise ending . . . An entertaining mystery with a satirical tone."

—*Booklist*

"Juliet Applebaum is smart, fearless, and completely candid about life as a full-time mom with a penchant for part-time detective work. Kinsey Millhone would approve."

—Sue Grafton

NURSERY CRIMES

"[Juiet is] a lot like Elizabeth Peters's warm and humorous Amelia Peabody—a brassy, funny, quick-witted protagonist."

—*Houston Chronicle*

"A delightful debut filled with quirky, engaging characters, sharp wit, and vivid prose."

—Judith Kelman, author of *After the Fall*

"[Waldman] derives humorous mileage fom Juliet's 'epicurean' cravings, wardrobe dilemmas, night-owl husband, and obvious delight in adventure." —*Library Journal*

Berkley Prime Crime books by Ayelet Waldman

NURSERY CRIMES
THE BIG NAP
A PLAYDATE WITH DEATH
DEATH GETS A TIME-OUT
MURDER PLAYS HOUSE
THE CRADLE ROBBERS
BYE-BYE, BLACK SHEEP

BYE-BYE, BLACK SHEEP

Ayelet Waldman

BERKLEY PRIME CRIME, NEW YORK

THE BERKLEY PUBLISHING GROUP
Published by the Penguin Group
Penguin Group (USA) Inc.
375 Hudson Street, New York, New York 10014, USA
Penguin Group (Canada), 90 Eglinton Avenue East, Suite 700, Toronto, Ontario M4P 2Y3, Canada
(a division of Pearson Penguin Canada Inc.)
Penguin Books Ltd., 80 Strand, London WC2R 0RL, England
Penguin Group Ireland, 25 St. Stephen's Green, Dublin 2, Ireland (a division of Penguin Books Ltd.)
Penguin Group (Australia), 250 Camberwell Road, Camberwell, Victoria 3124, Australia
(a division of Pearson Australia Group Pty. Ltd.)
Penguin Books India Pvt. Ltd., 11 Community Centre, Panchsheel Park, New Delhi—110 017, India
Penguin Group (NZ), 67 Apollo Drive, Rosedale, North Shore 0745, Auckland, New Zealand
(a division of Pearson New Zealand Ltd.)
Penguin Books (South Africa) (Pty.) Ltd., 24 Sturdee Avenue, Rosebank, Johannesburg 2196,
South Africa

Penguin Books Ltd., Registered Offices: 80 Strand, London WC2R 0RL, England

BYE-BYE, BLACK SHEEP

A Berkley Prime Crime Book / published by arrangement with the author

PRINTING HISTORY
Berkley hardcover edition / August 2006
Berkley Prime Crime mass-market edition / July 2007

Cover art by Lisa Desimini.
Cover design by Steven Ferlauto.

ISBN: 978-0-425-21639-2

BERKLEY® PRIME CRIME
Berkley Prime Crime Books are published by The Berkley Publishing Group,
a division of Penguin Group (USA) Inc.,
375 Hudson Street, New York, New York 10014.
The name BERKLEY PRIME CRIME and the BERKLEY PRIME CRIME design are trademarks belonging to Penguin Group (USA) Inc.

PRINTED IN THE UNITED STATES OF AMERICA

10 9 8 7 6 5 4 3 2 1

To Mary Evans

Acknowledgments

This novel was written at Hedgebrook, a retreat for women writers. I am eternally grateful to that marvelous place and its incomparable staff for the gift of time, solitude, peace, and space.

Thanks to Tsan Abrahamson, Kristina Larsen, and Devin McIntyre.

And to the wonderful people at Berkley: Leslie Gelbman, Abigail Thompson, Susan Allison, Donita Dooley, Sharon Gamboa, Don Rieck, Michelle Vega, and Trish Weyenberg. And especially Natalee Rosenstein.

One

I fingerprinted my seven-year-old daughter because they made me. I didn't want to do it. It made me uncomfortable to dot her plump thumbs on the little pad of ink and roll them on the stiff white card. Her left thumb was soggy and creased from its night's sleep tucked firmly against the roof of her mouth, so the print it left was smeared and almost unreadable.

"Okay, all done. Go wash your hands," I said, as I tucked the card back into its plastic jacket.

"My turn," my son, Isaac, said.

I shook my head. "We don't need to do one for you."

"But I want to do it, too."

"Sorry, honey."

Ruby turned from the kitchen sink where she was lathering up her hands with an excess of dishwashing liquid. "It's only for big kids," she said.

"Why?" he said.

She gave a disdainful shake of her carrot-colored curls. "Because."

"Why does she get to do it?" he demanded. "She's not so big."

I said, "Because her teacher said we had to."

"It's for my own protection," Ruby said, parroting the words of the kindly Los Angeles Police Department officer who had come to her school and distributed the cards. "It's so that if I get stolen Mama and Daddy can get me back."

Isaac's lower lip began to tremble and glycerin tears gathered on his eyelashes. "But I want to come back, too. It's not fair."

This was precisely why I hadn't wanted to do this in the first place. This was why I object on principle to the whole notion of educating small children about abduction and kidnapping. The fear that our children will be stolen from us has become a national obsession. We watch the stories of Polly and Amber's abductions on television, and torture ourselves by imagining the last hours of their lives. We instruct our children to avoid contact with those they don't know, never to speak to strangers, never to get into the car with a stranger, even if he asks them to help him with his sick puppy, or if he tells them that Mommy sent him to pick them up because something terrible has happened. We teach them about "bad touches" and "good touches." And now it seems we fingerprint them and file the cards away, not, as Ruby says, so we can find them if they are snatched, because if they are found we would know them. I fear that these cards have one use only. They are used to identify the bodies.

All this fear, all this anxiety and, when population is factored into the analysis, the rates of stranger-abduction have remained constant over the years. It is no more likely that our children will be stolen and murdered than it was when I was small, in the late 1970s. No more likely, despite the fact that back then we all had the run of our neighborhoods, riding our bikes through the streets, playing kick the can and hide-and-seek until dark.

The cost of this parental apprehension is high. I see it now in Isaac's face as he struggles to understand from whom his sister is being protected and why he is not lucky enough to dabble in black ink to earn the same defense. I see it in Ruby's understanding of a world that, infected by the unease of the adults around her, now includes hordes of malicious strangers intent on doing her harm.

"I want to do my fingerprints," Isaac wailed.

Sadie, who at eight months old is always ready to lend her voice to any catastrophe, looked up from her pile of Cheerios and let loose with a full-throated cry.

It's important for a parent to stand firm, to be consistent in her rules. Once a mother makes a decision, she must stick to it, whatever the cost. Otherwise the child learns only that a tantrum is the best method to get his way.

"Okay, okay," I said. "I'll get another card from Ruby's teacher and we'll do your fingerprints tonight. Stop screaming, or you'll wake up Daddy."

Another stellar moment in the annals of Juliet Applebaum, bad mother.

But I really didn't want the kids to wake Peter up. My husband is a screenwriter, responsible for such classics of American cinema as *The Cannibal's Vacation* and *Flesh-eaters I*, *II*, and *III*. With an animated version of his cannibal series in production, he had earned himself a little room to experiment with something new. The cartoon cannibals would pay the mortgage on our rundown 1926 Hollywood Hills pile of a house for a little while, at least until the series was canceled, so Peter didn't have to churn out another horror movie right away. I still wasn't earning very much as a private investigator, although the month before had been unusually lucrative for me and my partner. In that one month I'd brought home almost as much working part-time as I had when I was working ten hours a day or more as a federal public defender. That was a significant improvement over the months when the business had *cost* me money.

Peter was making the most of the opportunity his series had bought him, and had been up until close to four A.M. hashing out the structural problems of Act II of a screenplay entirely unlike anything he'd ever done before.

He was writing a kung fu movie.

Some people think my husband is a strange guy, although I take issue with that. I think most men of his generation harbor a perhaps unhealthy obsession with comic books, action figures, and other detritus of their childhoods. Peter's passion for vintage Mego action figures and DC 100-Page Super Spectaculars stems from a slightly different place from most of the guys he hangs out with at Hi De Ho Comics. He has the complete run of twelve-inch G.I. Joes, from 1964 to 1976, with a particular interest in Kung Fu Grip and Life-Like Hair, not because those are the toys he played with when he was a little boy, but because those are the toys he desired but did not own. It's nostalgia, but nostalgia for unfulfilled passions. Peter grew up in Cincinnati, Ohio, a city quite a bit closer to Appalachia than most people realize. It's as far as his parents got when they climbed up out of the holler and down off the mountain. They made it to the city, but the city didn't make much of them, and there was never enough money to go around, certainly not enough for toys. Peter never had a G.I. Joe. He had a couple of G.I. Joe outfits, and a knock-off military doll from a discount store that was called something like Army Jack, but he never had the real thing. He's making up for lost time, now. I think his collection is up to around thirty, and those are just the G.I. Joes. I couldn't even begin to count the other vintage superhero dolls. And then there are the Star Wars action figures.

He's good at sharing, though. There are definitely figures he insists on keeping in their original blister packs, but there are plenty of others he lets the kids play with. Peter's office is an authentic dungeon in the basement of our house, complete with handcuffs bolted to the wall and an antique vaulting horse that still bears the marks of leather straps and cords (either the movie star who built our house, Ramon Navarro, had something of a predilection for the sadomasochistic or he'd been taken for a ride by an insane interior decorator). It is a paradise of toys and dolls.

Another of Peter's loves is Hong Kong martial arts movies. His favorite director is Yuen Woo-ping, the Master. Peter says his name with an awed reverence, the kind you might reserve for the Pope if you were a devout Catholic, or for Leonard Nimoy if you spent your weekends at *Star Trek* conventions, in uniform, wearing a pair of fake pointed ears. Peter's goal with this current project was to write a script worthy of the Master, or of Tsui Hark or King Hu or one of the other Hong Kong auteurs whose light touch and balletic grace with a sword and nunchaku he so admires.

That morning, I had to keep the kids quiet so Peter could get a decent morning's sleep after a hard night's work. Then I had to get the kids out the door for school, and get myself and Sadie down to Westminster, to my partner Al Hockey's garage, from which we ran our suddenly not-entirely-unprofitable business. Al and I met when he was an investigator for the federal public defender and I was a newbie lawyer. He'd helped me get through my first investigations, and I'd earned his respect, despite my manifold screwups. He liked me, he said, because I was "game." When I left the office to stay home with my kids, Al warned me that I wasn't going to make it as a stay-at-home mom. "You'll be bored in about three weeks," he said. He was wrong. Very wrong.

It took three days. Three days of Gymboree and Mommy & Me and story time at the library. Three days of walking the neighborhood pushing my stroller and desperately trying to meet other moms with kids more or less the same age. Three days of driving from one playground to the other, making a thorough and scientific comparison of the various swings and teeter-totters. After three days I was pulling my hair out. I just wasn't suited to that kind of life. I wasn't one of those moms who could be happy spending soporific hours in the park discussing theories of child development and swapping potty-training tips. I love my kids, but spending eighteen hours a day alone with them was turning me into a psychotic bitch with a vocabulary more constricted than the average toddler. I stuck it out, though, for years, doing my best to drown my sorrows in whipped mochas and crumb cake.

I had finally decided that neither my ass nor my ambitions could hack it anymore, when Al showed up with the idea of starting an investigative agency. He said I could work a few hours a day, just to occupy my mind with something other than which breast pump was the most effective and whether or not exposure to television would cause my children to develop attention deficit disorder.

(The answer to that last question, by the way, is yes. Yes, of çourse, but so what? It's worth it. Nothing buys a mother a more peaceful eighty-four minutes than the DVD of *The Lion King*.)

Two

WHEN I got to the garage I found Al and our assistant, Chiki Rodriguez, dancing anxious attendance on a very unusual guest. The first thing I noticed was that she was tall; even sitting down she seemed to tower over Chiki. She stared down at the top of his head as he refilled her coffee cup. The second thing I noticed was the size of her feet. She had one leg crossed over the other, and a boat of a parrot green pump dangled from her long toes. The shoes, with their chrome spike heels glinting in the harsh light of the fluorescent bulbs, were easily a size thirteen.

"Juliet," Al said. "Miss Heavenly has been waiting for you."

I passed Sadie from my hip to Chiki's waiting arms and extended my hand. The woman's chartreuse acrylic nails added a good two inches to what were already vast hands and, as my palm disappeared into hers, I felt like a miniature schnauzer giving a paw to her mistress. The woman's handshake was firm, but not bone-crushing. She was clearly adept at restraining the force of her grip. I looked up from her hand to her face. It was covered with a thick layer of creamy foundation, fluttery false eyelashes, and eye shadow that precisely matched the sparkling green of her nails. I'm embarrassed to say that it was only at that moment, as I was staring at the theatrical makeup applied with a clearly practiced hand, that I realized that Miss Heavenly was a man. Or had been, at one point in her life.

"I'm Juliet Applebaum," I said. "How can I help you?"

Sadie squawked and I turned to Chiki. "Will you take her to Jeanelle for me?"

A few months before, when it became clear that Sadie was no longer going to sit quietly in her bouncy seat while I worked, I had confronted the dilemma of every working mother: What was I going to do about child-care? Most days I worked only during the hours that the older kids were at school, but I still needed someone to watch Sadie between carpools if I was going to get anything done. I had a couple of disastrous interviews with nannies sent over by a nanny search service. One woman informed me that she required a scent-free environment and would only work for me if I removed all products with fragrances—including, but not limited to, detergent, soap, and cleaning supplies—from my house, my baby, and my person. This was a somewhat ironic request, as this particular nanny applicant might have been *scent*-free, but she was sure as shooting not *odor*-free. Another prospective nanny took one look at my house and my three children, one of whom was, at the time, busily trying to resuscitate a dead pet banana slug named Francisco, and declined the job. Taking pity on me and on her husband's fledgling business, Al's wife, Jeanelle, had offered to help out a few hours a day. I'd resisted at first, worried about taking advantage of her, but she genuinely seemed to enjoy Sadie's company. I'd also offered pay her, which she graciously declined, informing me gently that I could not afford her.

Chiki disappeared into the house with Sadie and I turned back to my guest. She was adjusting the collar of her ruffled blouse and I noticed that her cleavage swelled seductively in the gap of the plunging neckline. The skin of her chest was the smooth, clear brown of maple syrup, darker and more lustrous than her face under all the makeup. She noticed my gaze and smiled.

"Oh, they're real, honey," she said. "I grew these girls all by myself." She cupped her breasts with her hands. I heard a strangled groan and turned to Al. He was fairly purple with embarrassment.

"Why don't I take Miss Heavenly inside the house," I said. "We'll talk in the living room, and you can get on with the Fanswatler search." We had an assignment from a film studio to work on a movie called *The Amazing Adventures of Arthur Fanswatler*. Unfortunately, an actual person named Arthur Fanswatler had come to light, a docent at the Victoria and Albert Museum in London. With a name this bizarre, the studio can protect itself from litigation by tracking down three or more people who share the name, thus putting it in the realm of the unusual but not unique. We were being paid a fee of ten thousand dollars to track down two more Arthur Fanswatlers.

"No, you stay here," Al said. "I'll work inside." He took off through the door leading to the house.

Miss Heavenly shook her head. "He's not one for the ladies, now, is he?"

I considered explaining to her that my partner is a traditional libertarian, and thus believes wholeheartedly in an individual's right to choose to behave and dress in any manner he or she pleases. Moreover, he's a conspiracy theorist with an arsenal that rivals that of David Koresh, and a long history of militia activity, so he not only believes in her right to be who she is, but would go to battle to protect it. But he's an old-fashioned, macho kind of guy, and however much he pontificates about individual liberty, a hulking transvestite in a skintight leather skirt and Diana Ross wig is just going to freak him out.

I shrugged. "So, what can I do for you?"

"You know my cousin, Pauline. She goes by Sister Pauline."

"Of course I do." A few months before I had worked on a case where Sister Pauline played a role. "How is she doing?"

"Oh, she's good. She's doing real good with the baby and all."

"That's great. I'm so glad."

"She told me what you did for her, and when she

found out about my little sister she said, 'You just go on and see Juliet. She'll help you out.' So here I am."

I settled myself behind my desk and woke up my laptop. "What's going on with your sister?" I said as I opened a blank screen and began typing.

"She was killed."

My fingers paused over the keyboard. "I'm so sorry," I said.

She blinked a few times. Waterproof or not, that much mascara would not have survived tears, and she knew it. "I want you to find the man who did it."

"Miss Heavenly," I began.

"Oh, you can just call me Heavenly. It's your friend who kept calling me Miss. My name is just Heavenly. One word, no last name. Like Cher and Madonna."

"Heavenly," I said, "Al and I don't really investigate murders. That's a job for the police. I can help you in your dealings with the police, give you advice and that kind of thing, but I can't do the investigation for them."

The truth was that though Al and I had investigated more than our share of murders, and had a clearance rate as good or better than the LAPD homicide squad, murder cases were just not what we looked to get involved in. We had an entirely different kind of caseload. We did mitigation investigations for defense attorneys, researching a defendant's history and family to find evidence to prevent the jury from imposing a death sentence. We did insurance investigations, and we had a lucrative contract with an attorney to various Hollywood stars, keeping the messes his clients made for themselves from turning into real disasters. Now we were doing our first job for a film studio. That was the kind of work we needed to stay in business—corporate clients, law firms, no emotional attachment, and the bills paid on time.

A murder investigation requires sophisticated investigative tools. Fingerprints, DNA, and crime-scene analysis are just the beginning. Access to crime-scene photographs and the postmortem report is almost always necessary to resolve a case, as is access to the witnesses. Homicides are most often solved by a sophisticated examination and assessment of the physical evidence, including DNA markings, ballistics reports, and hair and fiber analyses (although these last are iffy at best. Many a person has gone to jail or even faced execution based on a faulty hair analysis.) We just don't have the resources for that, and there are only so many favors Al can call in from the guys he used to work with in the LAPD.

"The police haven't helped us," Heavenly said. She uncrossed her legs and leaned forward in her chair, splaying her large hands out on my desk. "My baby sister was killed six months ago, and the police have done nothing." Her voice shook. "Nothing, you hear? They can't be bothered with her. My mother saw the detectives *once*, when they came by the house to tell her Violetta was dead. I've been calling the case officer for months. When he deigns to return my calls, he has nothing to say."

I frowned. If there's one thing I'm a sucker for, it's a story about police incompetence or negligence. It just burns me up. "What's the case officer's name?" I said.

She reached into her green faux crocodile purse, pulled

out a worn and bent business card, and handed it to me. I took the card and put it on our brand-new copy machine. I made two copies, one for me and one for Al.

"I'll tell you what," I said, despite the fact that my better instincts were telling me to avoid this case like the plague. I've never done a very good job of paying attention to those little voices in my head. "I'm not sure I can help you, but the least I can do is give this Detective . . ." I glanced down at the card. "Detective Jarin a call, and see what's going on with their investigation."

"Thank you so much," Heavenly said, and now she did tear up. She raised her face to the ceiling to keep the tears from spilling and, grabbing a tissue from the box on my desk, began dabbing at her eyes.

I said, "I'm going to need to hear about Violetta. If you can bear it, tell me as many details of the crime as you know."

The story Heavenly told was sordid and sad. Her younger sister, the youngest girl in a family of seven siblings, had slipped into a life of drug use and prostitution. "She wasn't the first of my sisters to go that way," Heavenly said. "We had it hard growing up. There was never any money in our house, and I think this seemed like easy money to them. My older sister Annette was on the streets for years before she died of AIDS. I have two brothers in prison, one for cocaine and one for jacking a car."

"Wow," I said, for lack of anything better.

"But my other sister Chantelle, she's an RN and her husband's a doctor. He's doing a surgical residency at UCLA. My youngest brother, Ronnie, he's a senior at UC

San Diego. He wants to go into computers. Chantelle, Ronnie, and I, we came out all right."

My face must have betrayed something because she shook her head at me, obviously disappointed. "You don't think I'm all right?"

"No, no, of course I do," I stammered. "I mean, I think you're just fine."

"I'll have you know that I have a good job, a steady boyfriend, I own my own home, as well as two rental properties, and I'm supporting not just myself and my mother, but Ronnie, too. I have paid every dime of that boy's tuition. Not to mention supporting Annette's two girls and Violetta's son, Vashon. The children live with my mother, but I'm the one who pays everyone's bills."

By now I was blushing furiously. "I apologize. I didn't mean anything. Really I didn't."

She shifted in her chair, not so easily mollified.

"Tell me more about Violetta," I said. "First of all, what was her last name?"

"Spees."

"Where did she live?"

"Wherever she could. With me or my mother when she was clean, and in SROs on the South Side when she was using, which was most of the time. Even when she was gone, I'd put twenty dollars a month on her cell phone, just so she could call us every once in a while. So we'd know she was okay." She began blinking again, determined not to risk her makeup.

"Would you write your mother's phone number and address down here for me?" I pushed a small pad of paper across the desk. "And yours, too, so I know where to reach you."

After she returned it to me I glanced at it. Her mother's name was Corentine Spees. Heavenly's address was in West Hollywood, not too far from my old house in Hancock Park.

"Do you know anything about who Violetta's friends were? Who she hung around with?"

She shrugged. "No. I know she worked Figueroa, at Eighty-fourth Street. That was her corner. If I needed to see her I could always find her there."

I made quick notes on my laptop. That grim area of South Central Los Angeles, with its hot-sheet motels and prostitutes vying with drug dealers for space on the street corners, was a place that the rest of the city did its best to pretend wasn't there, ignoring the violence and misery, recalling its existence only when it spilled past the designated borders.

"Can you tell me a little about her murder?" I said.

Heavenly seemed to steel herself. "They found her body dumped in an alley. She was beat up bad. The medical examiner said she died of a cerebral hemorrhage."

"You saw the autopsy report? Do you have it?"

Heavenly shook her head. "The funeral director told me. I think he thought it would be a comfort to me to know that she was unconscious when she died. And I think he wanted to explain why she looked . . . well, why he couldn't make her look better. Her head was sort of . . ." Heavenly paused and pressed her fingertips to the corners of her eyes. "The side of her face . . . I thought he should have been able to do a better job with that."

"I'm so sorry," I said. "That must have made everything that much worse."

Heavenly reacted the way I do when I'm upset and someone is sympathetic. She started to cry.

"Damn it," she said. "I was *not* planning on breaking down in here."

"You lost your sister in a horrible way. Of course it makes you cry. Maybe you can tell me a little bit about her before we talk any more about what happened to her. You said she had a son?"

Heavenly nodded. "Vashon. He's seven years old. He's a good boy, a little wild. He misses his mama. You know."

"Was he living with her when she died?"

"No, he's been with our mother since he was born. Violetta was on the street when she had him. She did her best to clean up while she was pregnant, but it was hard for her. She couldn't get into a drug treatment program; she tried, but we couldn't find one that would accept a pregnant woman. She was a fighter, Violetta, and she fought her urges for Vashon's sake. She did the best she could."

"Do you know who Vashon's father is?"

Heavenly gave a short, cynical bark of laughter. "Honey, I told you, Violetta worked the streets. Only the Lord in heaven knows who that boy's father is. I'll tell you what, though, I'd put my money on him being a white man. Vashon's a cup of coffee with a good-sized dollop of cream."

"Was Violetta seeing anybody else that you know of?"

Heavenly shrugged.

"What drugs was she using?"

"What drugs *wasn't* she using? She smoked crack. And when she had some money, she shot dope, too. She did meth once in a while, although I don't think it was her favorite. Vi always said crank was a white man's high."

Heavenly had collected herself, her eyes were dry, and I wished I didn't have to go back to asking about Violetta's murder, but there was no way around it. I put my laptop to one side, not wanting to be staring at my computer screen, taking notes like some unsympathetic stenographer. "Heavenly, I'm so sorry to ask this, but can you tell me if Violetta was sexually assaulted before she was killed?"

"They wouldn't say so for sure, only that they found evidence of sexual contact." Heavenly shook her head, angrily. "I know she was raped. If some little white girl had been found tossed behind a Dumpster on Santa Monica Boulevard the cops wouldn't dare suggest it was anything but rape."

If some little white girl had been tossed behind a Dumpster on Santa Monica Boulevard you can be sure it would have been front-page news in the *L.A. Times* and the top story on the local news. I wouldn't have been hearing about it for the first time today.

"Did the police have any suspects at the time, anyone they were looking at?"

Heavenly shrugged. "The most I could get out of the detective was that they were operating on the assumption that it was a trick who killed her."

"Did she keep any kind of a record of her regular

clients?" I didn't have high hopes for this. She was a streetwalker, not a thousand-dollar-a-night prostitute with a BlackBerry and an answering service. I was guessing that her regulars knew what corner to find her on, and if she was busy when they pulled up, they either called over another girl, or waited ten minutes until Violetta was free.

Heavenly just shook her head.

"Okay," I said. "I'll give the detective a call. See what's going on with the investigation at this point. At the very least I can try to light a fire under him."

Heavenly reached for her crocodile purse and unsnapped it. "How does this work?" she asked. "Do I pay you by the hour or is it a flat fee?"

I held up my hand to stop her. "No, no. I'm not going to take your money just to call the detective. Depending on what I find out, we can decide what Al and I can do for you, if there's any point to hiring us. We'll talk about money then. We usually take a small retainer against the ultimate fee, and after that we bill by the hour." I handed her the rate sheet that Jeanelle had designed for Al and me once she realized that our approach to charging our client billing wasn't exactly what she could have wished. It was printed on fine stock in fourteen-point font. Big enough not to miss the point. It cost money to hire us. A lot of money. I could pretty much imagine what Jeanelle would say when she found out that I had promised a client an hour or two of free work.

"Those are our normal rates," I said. "But there's some flexibility there." Jeanelle was going to kill me.

Heavenly unfolded herself from the chair and rose to

her feet. In her four-inch heels she was a good six and a half feet tall. The oily curls of her wig just missed the hanging light fixture in the middle of our ceiling, and at just over five feet tall I barely came up to her artfully displayed bosom. She had a perfect view of the brown roots of my red hair.

Once again my hand was swallowed up by her huge one. I watched as she walked out the door and marveled at the smoothness of her step in her spike heels. I have a weakness for shoes, one that I have been known to indulge. My own closet has more than its share of stilettos in various hues. However, I've never done more than mince in my shoes. I wondered how many years of practice it took to acquire such a confident stride.

Three

AFTER Heavenly left, Al stuck his head into the garage. "All clear?" he said. At my nod he and Chiki came back in and resumed their seats.

I shook my head at him "You sure have some delicate sensibilities for an ex-cop. And here I thought you'd 'seen it all.' " I put ostentatious quotation marks around the last phrase. It was one of Al's favorites and, until this moment, I'd actually figured it for true.

Al was a cop for a couple of decades, until he was gut shot while on a routine call. Even after he'd been wounded he'd tried to stay on, but he turned out to be constitutionally incapable of spending his life behind a desk and leaving the fieldwork to the other guys. He'd taken early retirement and become an investigator for the federal defender's office.

"I've seen transvestites before," Al said. "I've arrested transvestites before."

"For what?"

He shrugged. "You know, this and that."

"Oh, great. You've rousted transvestites all across the city, but you can't stand the idea of sitting in the same room with one. Well, I'll have you know that not only is Heavenly a lovely woman, but she's also a client."

"I'll sit down with any paying client, no matter who they are," Al said. The cracked leather cushion of his chair gave a little sigh as he settled into it, and the oak creaked and groaned under his substantial weight. Someday that chair was just going to buckle under and collapse in a pile of splintered twigs.

I refrained from telling him that Heavenly wasn't paying us anything yet, and even if she did hire us, it was unlikely that I was going to have the nerve to charge her anything like our regular fee.

"Here," Al said, handing me a pile of papers. "You do Australia. I'm going to try the Finnish police. My guy at Interpol turned up a possible arrest record for an Arthur Fanswatler in Helsinki."

I pulled out the list of Australian area codes. Why the online services don't have a more accurate record of listed phone numbers is beyond me. "You really get off on saying that, don't you?" I said.

"Saying what?"

"My guy at Interpol."

Al laughed. His "guy" was a computer analyst and a friend of Chiki's. Our assistant was on supervised release from federal prison for computer fraud, for hacking the INS system. This was back before the INS had been absorbed into the Department of Homeland Security and I guess security hadn't been as tight as it is now. Or maybe it's still just as easy to hack into, who knows? Chiki was the Robin Hood of East L.A., giving out green cards to people he thought deserved them. He hadn't made a dime off his exploits, and he'd done it all with a 28k modem and an old Mac Plus that he'd modified himself. When his case came across the Interpol analyst's desk, the guy had been so impressed that in addition to adding Chiki's name to the list of known computer hackers and security risks, he'd sent him a fan letter. Chiki had been serving the second year of his federal sentence when he got the letter, and they immediately became fast friends and correspondents. Once Chiki started working for us, François had been happy to lend us the occasional hand.

After leaving word for Detective Jarin, the case officer assigned to Violetta's homicide, I busied myself calling Australian operators.

Right before I had to leave to pick up the kids from school, Al gave a bellow and pumped his fist in the air.

"Got him!" he said. "Arthur Fanswatler, resident of Helsinki. Date of birth, January 11, 1954. Investigated in 2002 on suspicion of downloading kiddie porn. No charges filed."

I shuddered. "Maybe the studio will change their

minds about the name once they realize that one of their Fanswatlers is a pedophile."

"Not our problem," Al said. "One down, one to go."

By then I was running late for carpool and had barely enough time to nurse Sadie before shoving her into her carseat and tearing up the 5 to make the rounds of the kids' schools. I was only five minutes late for Isaac, but there was construction on La Brea Boulevard and a cop sitting right where I'd hoped to make an illegal left turn. I arrived at Ruby's school only nine minutes late by my watch, but eleven by her teachers. I knew from past experience that there was no appeals process, so I just gritted my teeth and paid the fine.

Ruby was most displeased by my tardiness. She had her backpack on her back and was tapping one purple-booted toe. "You're late."

"Don't I know it. Eleven bucks out of my pocket. I'm sorry, kiddo, but there was terrible traffic. And you know it takes a long time to get here from Westminster."

"So leave earlier."

"Ruby!" I said, but there wasn't much heart in my rebuke. She did, after all, have a point.

"In case you forgot," she said as she clambered into her booster seat. "Madeline is coming over for a playdate. At three." She pushed back her sleeve and studied her Tinkerbell watch. "That's in fifteen minutes."

"I didn't forget. We'll make it." But of course I had forgotten. It's hard enough to keep my own schedule straight, let alone my daughter's. What with gymnastics and Mad Science, Tae Kwon Do, and Hebrew school, I spent most of my time in the car. And when I wasn't driving her to an activity, I was either taking her to or hosting a playdate.

I hate the very idea of playdates. Our parents never set up playdates for us. They sent us "out to play." What child nowadays goes out to play? What child ambles over to a neighbor's house, rings the doorbell, and asks if Sally or Susie can come out and play? All of us parents are so fearful of strangers wandering through our neighborhoods, even in neighborhoods like mine that are full of big houses nestled in well-tended gardens. We barely even let our children out within the confines of our fenced backyards. Instead we schedule playdates, supervising their social lives and activity calendars like social secretaries.

"I want a playdate, too," Isaac said.

"I didn't set one up for you today, little man," I said.

"It's not fair! Ruby gets a playdate and I don't."

A few months ago I had decided to stop responding to the kids' claims of injustice with a bitter "life's not fair." It might be true, but it doesn't do much by way of convincing them of the correctness of my position. This time, I tried something my mother used to do that had been pretty effective when I was a kid. I ignored him and turned on the radio.

Madeline and her mother were waiting for us on our front steps because of course we didn't make it home by three. As I labored to the door with Sadie dangling from one arm, and the kids' backpacks and my purse from the other, I plastered a bright and hospitable smile on my face.

"I'm so sorry we're late," I said. "Traffic. But why didn't you just ring the bell? Peter should be home."

"We did ring the bell," Madeline said. "We rang it and rang it."

"That's enough, Maddy," her mother said. "I told you Ruby would be here sooner or later. She was worried Ruby's mommy had forgotten all about us, weren't you, sweetie?"

Maddy nodded.

So Maddy and her mom were on time. Big Deal. Donna Jorgenson Farrell had exactly one child, a live-in nanny, and no job. Unless her Pilates class ran over, she was destined never to be late to anything.

"I can't wait to see what you've done with the house," Donna said as we walked through the door, down the front hall, and into the ballroom. The kids' bikes were tossed in a corner of the empty room, and there was a little pile of broken parquet flooring pieces that Sadie had gathered on one of her foraging expeditions.

Donna hid her moue of disapproval with a gay little laugh. "Gosh, it must be so hard to decide what to do with a room this size."

"We're debating between a pool hall and a roller rink."

"Oh, how interesting."

I ushered Donna into the kitchen while the girls ran off to Ruby's room, Isaac in their wake. "Can I get you something to drink or do you need to get going?" I said hopefully.

"Oh no, there's nowhere I need to be. I'm happy to

stay and help with the girls. And I'd love an iced green tea, if that's not too much trouble," she said.

I gave what I hope was a not too sickly grin. "No trouble at all." I set about rummaging through my cabinets, steeping a cup of tea and pouring it over ice. I will never understand these mothers who insist on hanging around for playdates. They turn what might otherwise be an easy afternoon into an endless round of small talk and hostess duties. Here my oldest daughter was pleasurably distracted and instead of enjoying that relatively rare occasion, I had to sit here sipping tea with a virtual stranger. It would be one thing if we were friends. I'd gotten close to a number of the moms of kids in Ruby's preschool class, and could happily while away hours in their company. What with the two younger kids and work, I just hadn't had the time to make friends with the elementary school mommies. And now I was paying the price.

I probably would have liked Donna more if she wasn't so thin. And if she hadn't brought her own packets of sweetener in her purse. "We try not to take any sugar; it's really just a drug, you know. And this is the only natural sugar substitute out there. You ought to try it. I'll leave you a few packets, if you like."

I glanced down at the roll of fat spilling over the waistband of my pants. I'd recently started being able to get the zipper all the way up on my pre-pregnancy jeans and I'd celebrated by cramming myself into them nearly every day. I guess they didn't look quite as good as I'd hoped.

"Great," I said.

Donna clearly had no problem with the zipper of her cocoa suede slacks. Her midriff, revealed by her fetching little half-sweater, showed no evidence whatsoever of reproduction. She took a delicate sip of her tea and said, "I heard the most remarkable thing on the radio today. There is a company in Japan that will insert a small microchip under the skin of your pet, so that if it ever runs away they can track it on a global positioning system."

"They're putting LoJacks on dogs?"

"Isn't it remarkable? Apparently the only problem with the technology is that it won't work if it gets wet, but they're working on solving that. I think it's just terrific. I mean, if they can figure that little glitch out, there's no reason we can't use them for children. What's more important, right? A dog or a baby?"

"You want to insert a microchip into Madeline?"

Donna was so wrapped up in the possibilities she was describing that she did not hear the doubt in my voice. Or else she just ignored it. "Just think if poor Polly Klaas had had a microchip under her skin. They could have found her right away, before that man did anything to her."

"But wouldn't a kidnapper just cut it out? Wouldn't that be worse for the child?"

"Oh, I'm sure they're totally undetectable. They'd have to be."

I couldn't stop myself. I launched into my speech about how FBI statistics show no greater threat of child abduction now, in 2006, than thirty years ago, and how the real danger our children face is our own fear. I was really getting into it, describing the toll our restrictions take on our children's lives, pontificating about the dangers of raising children who've never experienced activities unmediated by adults, when I noticed Donna's face. Not that I'm unused to that particular expression of disapproval, but it does tend to stop a person in her tracks.

"Oh, but Juliet. Even if only one child a year is taken, you don't want that to be your child, do you? And consider what this means for when the girls are teenagers. We'll be able to know exactly where they are at all times. They'll never be able to lie to us."

"Like we lied to our parents?"

"Exactly!" she said, happy for me because I finally understood. "They'll never be able to go anywhere or do anything without us knowing exactly what they're up to."

"Well, that does sound like fun for them. And for us. I can't wait."

Four

IT looked like Detective Jarin wasn't particularly eager to return my call, and since Al was coming up to the city to see a man about a gun, I convinced him to accompany me to the 77th Division. I figured we would have more success in person than over voice mail.

Al and I met out in front of the station. He spent an anxious moment figuring out what to do with the original needlefire Damascus double-barrel smoothbore shotgun he had picked up for next to nothing from a man who had to unload his gun collection fast because he was convicted of a felony, and being found in possession of even a collectible could cost him five years in jail.

"I can't leave it in the car around here," Al said, clutching his new beloved to his chest and staring suspiciously around him. "This is figured European walnut I've got here."

The thing about most dangerous Los Angeles neighborhoods is that, with a few exceptions, they don't really look so awful. The strip malls have check-cashing joints and taquerias in the them, instead of boutiques and sushi bars, but a strip mall is more or less a strip mall. The houses don't look so bad, most of them, and it's only once you see the bars on the windows and the gates on the doors that you realize you're not in Mar Vista. The drug deals going down on the corners tend to give it away, too.

"You're parked right in front of a police station," I said. "You really think someone is going to smash your window to get an old gun?"

"First of all, this gun isn't old, it's antique. And second of all, you're damn straight I think someone is going to break in and steal it, police station or no police station. People want guns, that's a fact. They'll do anything to get them."

"I agree. That's why I think they shouldn't be so damn plentiful and easy to buy."

"Are we really going to have this discussion again?"

I followed him into the station and stayed quiet while he made nice with the desk sergeant. By the time Al got around to asking if Jarin was available and if the sergeant would hold his gun for him while he spoke to the detective, they were old friends. The officer was only too glad to give the detective a buzz. Buttering up cops is Al's specialty and one of his most important skills as an investigator.

Detective Phil Jarin was a slight man, with a hollow-cheeked face pitted with acne scars. His dusty blue sport jacket looked at least two sizes too big; it hung off his shoulders, the sleeves dropping to his knuckles. His fingernails were bitten so short that raw skin puffed over the nailbeds. It was clear from his suspicious glare that Al's brothers-in-arms bluster wasn't going to make any headway with this guy.

I took over, explaining why we were there and telling him that we hoped he'd give us an update on the case, some information that we could pass on to the family.

"What was the name of the victim?" Jarin said, rubbing one chewed finger against the side of his face and frowning.

"Violetta Spees."

He looked blank.

"African-American woman, about twenty-four years old? Murdered six months ago?"

He nodded. "Right, right. Blunt force trauma to the head. As I recall they had a long sheet on her over in vice."

Why wasn't I surprised that he couldn't remember her name but he easily recalled her history of prostitution?

We were standing at the front desk as the business of the precinct eddied around us. Just then two uniformed officers came in dragging a handcuffed young man between them. The prisoner was swearing at the cops and shouting about his rights. He wanted a lawyer, and he wanted one now.

"Do you think we might find somewhere a little more quiet to talk?" I asked.

"Who is it you represent?" the detective said.

I pulled out the retention letter I had had Heavenly sign before she left our office. "The victim's sister, Heavenly."

Detective Jarin cracked a small smile. "Oh sure. I remember that guy. He can call himself whatever he wants, but on his arrest record he's known as Henry Spees."

Neither Al nor I let our faces give away the fact that we hadn't known about our client's record.

Al said, "Well, he's a she nowadays, and going by the name Heavenly."

"You can come on to the back if you want," Detective Jarin said, "But there's not much I can show you. That case went nowhere, probably a John who got a little too worked up. The file's pretty thin."

He wasn't kidding. The index sheet at the front of the file had only a few things logged into it. Other than the initial report, a few photographs, an autopsy report, and a one-page supervisor's log, the file was empty. There was none of what you would expect to see in a complete homicide file. There were no records of an investigative canvass, the door-to-door inquiry and search for witnesses that is routine in a murder investigation. There were no witness statements or interview reports of any kind. The crime-scene report was brief, to say the least. A few sheets of paper and a checklist, most of which was blank. There were no supervisor assignment sheets. There was no news-clipping file.

"Nothing much here," Detective Jarin said.

"Would you consider showing us the autopsy report?" Al asked.

"You know I can't do that." He began leafing through it, angling his shoulder so we couldn't read it. We were sitting catty-corner to his small metal desk, on two chairs he had brought over. "I don't mind telling you what's in it. Basic stuff. Black female, abdominal scar, most likely from cesarean section, cause of death, like I said, blunt force trauma to the head. Ragged laceration on the back of the skull. Cranial fracture and cerebral hemorrhage. That's about it."

"Is there any indication of what she was hit with?" Al said.

He shrugged. "She might not have been hit at all."

"What do you mean?" I said.

"She could have been pushed or fallen against something. It's not real clear. Medical examiner thought it was one hard blow. That's as specific as he was willing to get."

"No paint or metal flakes in the wound?" I asked.

"Nope."

"Was there any evidence of sexual assault?"

"There was evidence of semen. We submitted it for analysis. Hmm." He sounded disturbed.

"What?" I said.

"Report never came back. Oh well," he shrugged. "Not much we could do with it, anyway."

"Any bruises or marks on her?" Al asked. "Abrasions that might indicate assault?"

"None," the detective said. "And her clothes weren't torn."

"He could have forced her to take off her clothes," I said.

"And then put them back on her once she was dead? Doubtful," Jarin said.

"He could have killed her after she was dressed."

The detective snapped the file closed. "Anyway, that's it," he said. "Not much more I can tell you."

"Didn't you interview any witnesses? Any of the other women who were working her corner? Maybe someone saw her get into a car that night."

He rose to his feet. "We did our investigation. There were no witnesses. At least none willing to talk. Now, I've got to get back to work. I've got a pile of live cases on my desk that need my attention."

Five

ONCE we had retrieved his gun, Al walked me to my car, despite my assurances that I could get myself down to the end of the block just fine. He ignored me, which is what he tends to do when I'm trying to prove a point that he thinks is silly.

I got in the driver's seat and turned the ignition on. Then I noticed that Al was still standing outside of my car. I rolled down the window. "It's bugging you, too, huh?" I said.

"I hate that crap," Al said. "That kind of shoddy police work."

"You think if she'd been a white girl they would have treated the case differently?"

He shrugged. "Are you asking me if they would have

investigated more thoroughly if she'd been a white hooker instead of a black one? I think the fact that she was a prostitute was why they gave it such low priority, but yeah, I think they would have made at least a symbolic effort for a white girl."

Al's feelings about race are unambiguous. Jeanelle is African-American, and Al is the father of two mixed-race daughters. He's seen racism directed at his family and at himself because of his family, and he doesn't have a lot of patience with it.

"What do you want to do?" I knew what I wanted to do. I was hoping he'd agree.

"Call the brother . . . er . . . the sister, and tell her we'll put a few hours into the case. We might as well see what we can turn up."

"I sort of told her we would give her a sliding scale rate."

He sighed. "Just do me a favor and don't tell Jeanelle. She's been so happy about us finally turning a real profit."

"*I'm* not going to tell Jeanelle. *I'm* not the one who can't keep a secret from Jeanelle."

Al said, "Should I run Henry Spees through the NCIC?" The federal public defender's investigative department has access to National Crime Information Center, a database of all offender records. Al's old colleagues in the office run names for us when we need them to.

I frowned. We had no business checking on the criminal record of our client. The alleged criminal record. "Yeah, you might as well," I said. "Just in case there's anything there we should know about."

He patted the roof of my car as if it were a pony he was sending on its way, and I headed off. I had barely enough time to make it down to Westminster to get Sadie before the kids had to be picked up from school. Sometimes it felt like I would only just get myself situated at my desk and it would already be carpool time again. And then there was the famous day that I got a flat tire in front of Isaac's preschool, and by the time the auto club showed up and changed it for me, it was time to pick the kid up again. Now that was a productive day.

After my swing through the city, I went home and fobbed the kids off on Peter. He was looking a little dazed but I figured they'd liven him up soon enough. Peter works at night, after the kids go to bed. He routinely starts at around ten or so, and by three in the morning I can usually count on him to be back in bed. The night before, he was still working when I got up with Sadie at six, and I had to force him to turn off the computer and go sleep.

"Take them to the park," I said. "I just nursed Sadie so she should be good for a few hours."

"Can we ride our scooters?" I heard Isaac asking as I took my laptop into our cavernous living room.

"Put your helmet on," Peter called after Isaac. "And your knee pads and wrist guards."

I called Heavenly. Grateful we had agreed to help her, she offered to gather her family together so I could interview them. I would have preferred to see them one by one, but I couldn't refuse her offer of a traditional Sunday dinner at her mother's house.

"And you should bring your baby," Heavenly said. "My mother's got the magic touch."

I sincerely hoped I wouldn't be forced to do that. It's hard enough to do a decent witness interview without a baby latched on to the breast. Not that I haven't done it before. I've done pretty much everything with a baby on the boob. Witness interviews, grocery shopping, online banking. I've even perfected a maneuver I call midflight refueling, where I nurse the baby while she's in her carseat and I'm sitting next to her, safely strapped into my own seatbelt. I haven't figured out how to do that when I'm the driver, though. But if I ever do, that's when I'll be totally liberated.

After I hung up the phone I did a web search. I was hoping to turn up some information on Violetta's murder. No such luck. I found some local crime reports of the discovery of the bodies of African-American female murder victims, but they were all old cases. There wasn't much I could do before meeting her family and seeing if any of them had more information than Heavenly. And of course, I was going to have to do what the police should have done and head over to Figueroa and Eighty-fourth some night soon, to see what the other girls on the corner could tell me. I wasn't looking forward to that.

The prospect of telling my husband that I was planning on ambling around one of the worst areas of Los Angeles after dark was not a pleasant one. Peter is in many ways the embodiment of the kind of egalitarian companion my girlfriends and I all imagined we would marry. He cooks, he's a great father, he's supportive of my career.

But he does have his failings, and one of them is a level of anxiety not so much about *what* I do as about my methods. He gets overprotective, like some kind of Arthurian knight. He thinks I put myself in the line of fire too easily, an accusation that I would consider unfair had I not once been shot while investigating a case. (It was just a leg wound, and had I not been pregnant, it wouldn't have been any big deal.) His gallantry is very sweet and romantic, and I know it's justified by my occasional irresponsibility, but what he doesn't understand is that doing this job well inevitably requires taking a certain amount of risk. I try to be reasonable about the risks I take and I'm careful about my children. They accompany me sometimes—I've even been known to use them as distraction, or a way to soften up a potential witness—but I would never put them in danger.

Anyway, it wasn't like I was planning on going into a war zone.

Six

Corentine Spees lived in the Thurgood Marshall Houses on Slausen. She'd lived most of her adult life in housing projects, and this one was certainly the best. She had a two-bedroom unit, which meant that the children were all piled into one room, but Heavenly had bought them a couple of bunk beds for Christmas a few years ago, so it wasn't too uncomfortable. There was a playground on the property that the children liked to play in; Corentine said if Vashon had his way he'd spend all his time watching the men and older boys playing basketball. She didn't like to let the little ones out on their own, not since the grandchild of a neighbor had been the unintended victim of a drive-by shooting. The gunmen had been aiming for one of the basketball players, but their aim was poor and they sprayed the swing set. The poor little thing had been shot right through the throat, Corentine told me. Seven years old and dead before she hit the ground.

Still, this was a better place to live than many, and Annette's girls were doing well in school. The older one, Tamika, was even in an after-school program for gifted children, the same program in which her uncle Ronnie had done so well. After the arrest of her oldest son—who'd been staying with her—on drug charges, Corentine had worried that the housing authority would take away her eligibility and toss her and the children out into the street, as they are permitted to do when one member of a family is involved in a drug crime. But so far that hadn't happened.

I was in the kitchen, mashing potatoes and chatting with Corentine and her daughter, Chantelle Green. They'd assigned me this task, I imagine, because it was the least likely for me to screw up. While I pounded away at the potatoes, working in the stick of margarine and handful of salt Corentine had tossed in the bowl, I asked them about their family and their lives. Corentine was a heavy woman, with small hands and a smooth, unlined face. She danced around her kitchen with a light-footed grace that belied her size. She wore her hair high and natural, tied back from her face and neck by a band of brightly woven fabric. She appeared to be of some indeterminate middle age, as young as fifty or as old as sixty-five. She had two gold teeth in the back of her mouth that flashed when she laughed.

Chantelle was a younger, thinner version of her mother. The same almond-shaped brown eyes, kewpie-doll lips, and skin the color of polished cherrywood, deep golden brown with just a hint of auburn. She had long hair, ironed straight. It hung in a stiff sheet, curling under precisely at her shoulders. Her hands, slicing the ham into neat rounds, were larger than her mother's, more like Heavenly's, long-fingered and capable. A nurse's hands.

"Oh Mama," she said, as she deftly carved the meat. "You'd just be so sad if you saw her." She had been telling her mother about bumping into an old friend from high school who as a girl had been in Chantelle's honors programs and on the cheerleading squad with her. Chantelle had met her at the hospital in the waiting room outside the WIC program. "She had at least five children with her, Mama. Five."

"Maybe she was watching her sister's babies."

Chantelle shook her head. "They were all her spitting image. Five children. And on WIC. Probably welfare, too."

"There's no shame in that, girl. Sometimes a person needs a little hand up, that's all."

"Oh Mama. You know she was a smart girl. She could have been anything she wanted. She could have gone to college. At one time she even said she was going to be a nurse like me. It's just a shame to see her like that. Her hair all nappy under a rag. Five children."

"You about done cutting up that ham?" Corentine said.

Heavenly, despite having adopted the gender of her sister, had not shed certain accustomed roles. She was not in the kitchen helping us put dinner on the table. Rather, she sat in the living room watching television with the children and her brother Ronnie, who had come up from San Diego especially to meet me. I imagine that there are some privileges of being a man, most notably the right to be served rather than to serve, that are difficult to sacrifice, even once one has changed an ill-suited body into one more appropriate to what's inside.

"Mama," Ruby said. "I'm hungry."

I turned to hush my daughter. Despite Heavenly's invitation, I had left the baby behind. Ruby had whined to join me, however, and I'd finally agreed. When we first arrived, Corentine and I had sent Vashon and Ruby into the children's room to play. They were close in age, and we figured they'd make easy enough companions. To Vashon's disgust, Ruby had soon enough rejected his boy toys and busied herself with the stuffed animals that Monisha, the younger of the two girls, kept on her bottom bunk. At twelve, Monisha was still young enough to be willing to play with Ruby, and the two of them had entertained themselves happily enough for a little while, before they got bored and joined the others in front of the TV.

"It'll just be another minute, baby," Corentine said. "Why don't you go tell everyone to wash their hands and come to the table."

Over dinner, with the children present, we limited ourselves to benign topics of conversation. The family told me about Violetta, but they talked of happier days, before they'd lost her to drugs and the street.

"She was such a good baby," Corentine said. "The easiest of all y'all. She never cried, never fussed. Even when she was a little girl she was so easygoing, such a quiet girl. Not like you two," she said, pointing at Chantelle and Heavenly. "Y'all were like a couple of cats, fighting over everything. You'd scratch each other so bad you'd draw blood."

At this Ruby looked up, a forkful of creamed corn halfway to her lips. I could almost see the little wheels in her head turning. *Blood! Now that's something I haven't managed. I've hit my brother, kicked him, even bitten him, but I've never succeeded in drawing blood.*

"Don't even think about it," I said to her.

She popped the corn into her mouth and gave me a yellow-toothed smile.

"She loved her boy," Heavenly said. "Vashon, I want you to remember that your mama loved you." Chantelle and Corentine nodded in agreement. Heavenly continued, "Why don't you tell Juliet what you remember about your mama?"

Vashon shrugged, his face bent over his plate.

"Go on, baby," his grandmother said. "You can tell about the time when Violetta was living with us and she got you that big birthday cake. It had all your favorite monsters from that movie on it. Remember that?"

"No," he said.

"Sure you do, honey," Heavenly said. "It was just this year, when you turned seven. Sure you remember."

"I don't remember it," he said.

Corentine said, "You do. Sure you do. Your mama was home for almost two weeks. She was doing so well, remember? She was looking for a job, and she went down to the welfare office to see about taking some classes in computers or something. Remember that? You were so proud of her."

"I don't remember nothing!" Vashon said, flinging his chair away from the table. "I don't remember her one little bit!" He threw down his fork and ran out of the room to his bedroom, slamming the door behind him.

"Oh," Corentine murmured, her plump face collapsing, suddenly showing all her years.

Chantelle said, "Girls, why don't you go into the kitchen and get yourself some dessert. Tamika, give everyone a piece of cake and take the girls into Nana's bedroom. You can watch TV in there."

"Come on, Ruby," Tamika said, extending a hand to my daughter to help her down from her chair. "We'll get some coconut cake and watch a movie. Auntie Chantelle always brings a coconut cake and a video for us to watch."

After the girls were gone we sat in silence for a moment. Then Chantelle said, "He's just grieving. He's going to be all right."

"Sure he will," Ronnie said. "That boy'll be all right."

Corentine said, "I just don't understand why he don't remember her cake. He just loved that cake so much." She pleated the tablecloth between her fingers.

"He remembers it, Mama," Heavenly said. "He remembers it just fine. He just can't talk about it now." She reached a long arm around her mother's shoulders and squeezed.

Chantelle clucked her tongue. "Mama, what he

remembers about his birthday party is that after she gave him the cake, Violetta drank herself sick, threw up all over the bathroom, cleaned out your pocketbook, and then went off with Deiondré, that friend of Ronnie's."

"He's not my friend," Ronnie said. "I just know him from the neighborhood. I didn't even invite him. He just came by to say hey to Vashon on his birthday, and Violetta grabbed him up."

I took out my notebook. "Deiondré?" I asked. "What's his last name?"

"Freeman," Ronnie said.

"Do you know his address?"

Corentine said, "His mother lives on the other side of the playground. I'm not sure what number, but Ronnie can show you."

"Do you think he might know something about what Violetta's life was like right before she died, who her friends were, that kind of thing?"

Ronnie shook his head. "He doesn't know nothing. She just went with him that once."

Heavenly said, "How do you know? I thought he wasn't a friend of yours? Since when have you been keeping tabs on Deiondré Freeman?"

Before this could turn into a full-fledged family squabble, I said, "I'll just ask him a question or two. Just in case." I hesitated. "I hope this won't be too hard on you, but in order to do a proper investigation I'll need to know as much about Violetta's life on the street as possible. Heavenly already told me that she spent most of her time on Figueroa."

Chantelle said, "At Eighty-fourth Street. That was her regular corner. She worked it for years. Before Annette got sick they were there together, and then Violetta just kept on, even after seeing what happened to her own sister."

"Annette died of the AIDS," Corentine said.

"Yes, Heavenly told me," I said. "Was she sick long before she died?"

Her mother stuck out her lower lip and it glowed bright pink against her face. "The AIDS took Annette so fast. She just got the pneumonia and went right away."

Chantelle said, "If I had known she'd had it I would have made sure she got the triple cocktail. My husband, Thomas, is a resident at UCLA medical school. He could have gotten her into a clinic. But it happened too fast. One day she showed up here with the worst cold, coughing so hard she could barely breathe. Mama called Heavenly and me, and we took her right to the emergency room. But it was too late. Her body was so weak, it just couldn't fight it. She passed that very night."

"When was this?" I asked.

"A little over a year ago," Heavenly said. "Just before Easter."

"And where was Violetta when all this was going on?"

Chantelle said, "My husband went out that night and brought her home. She stayed with Thomas and me through the funeral. And that's the last time I let her in my house." She turned to her mother. "I'm sorry, Mama, but you know it's true. She couldn't stay off the drugs for her own sister's funeral. I found her shooting up in my bathroom. In *my* bathroom. Thomas, he tried to convince her to check into a program; he said he would even pay for her to go to one of those nicer places. He's such a good man. It's not like we have the money for that kind of thing. But Violetta wouldn't even talk about it. Thomas and I had no choice; we threw her out and told her she couldn't come back." By the time she finished talking, Chantelle's face was flushed and a sheen of sweat stood out on her forehead. Her mother just stared down at the tablecloth.

"Where's Thomas tonight?" I asked.

"He's working. Like I said, he's a resident. He's on call more than he's off."

I nodded. "When was the next time you saw Violetta after you asked her to leave your house?"

"I saw her here, at Mama's house. She'd turn up every couple of months, looking for money, or a place to sleep. She knew Mama had a soft heart and wouldn't turn her away."

Heavenly said, "She did try to clean up every once in a while. Every six months or so she'd get clean. Once a couple of years ago she was clean for almost a month. But she'd always end up going back on the street. Sometimes she'd still be clean when she went back to work. She'd say she could be out there and not use, but once she hit the streets, we knew it would be over soon."

"Do any of you know the names of her friends, maybe women who knew her from the corner? Women who might have been out there with her on the night she was killed?"

Corentine said, "There was one girl she told me about once, a white girl. Violetta said she'd been in the movies. We were watching that movie, what's it called? With Julia Roberts. I can't remember it. But Violetta said this girl she knew was in the movie. We found her, too. We went back and forth on the VCR and we found her. She was a pretty girl, blond hair. Real nice looking. So sad to think she could have been a movie star and she ended up out there, doing that."

"Do you remember her name?"

"One of those names that starts with Mary. Mary something. Mary Elizabeth? Mary Alice? Like that."

I jotted down the details in my notebook. If the girl was still hanging out on Figueroa it wasn't going to be that hard to find her. The white prostitutes tended to congregate in other areas, like Hollywood on Sunset Boulevard. A white girl in South Central was going to be easy enough to track down.

"What about boyfriends, or regular clients? Heavenly told me she didn't know anything about Vashon's father, but do any of you?"

Corentine said, "She wouldn't tell us any of that. She knew how I felt about it. And Chantelle, too."

I turned to Ronnie. "What about you? Other than Deiondré, do you know any men your sister saw?"

"Huh?" he said. During the course of our conversation, he'd slowly shifted his chair around to face the television. Now, his attention was focused on *SpongeBob SquarePants*, not on my questions.

"Can you stop watching that for five minutes, please?"

Heavenly snapped. "She wants to know if you know any of Violetta's boyfriends."

"We don't have cable TV in the dorm," Ronnie said sheepishly. "Um, I don't know. She saw boys from the neighborhood way back when, but once she got turned out, I don't know. She didn't tell me about it, and I sure didn't ask."

I closed my notebook. "Well," I said. "You've given me a couple of leads to follow up on. Did you tell the police any of this back when they were investigating her murder?"

"They never asked," Corentine said.

Seven

RUBY and I got home to find Peter giving Sadie and Isaac their bath. Sadie was sitting in her little bath seat, her fat thighs jammed through the leg openings. She splashed with her hands, delighted with the sound of her palms slapping against the surface of the water. Isaac was lying with the back of his head submerged and his bony, bent knees poking up. I could not help but contrast my three children, so cosseted and spoiled, with Heavenly's nieces and nephews, their mothers horribly dead, their grandmother's and aunts' love and concern and their own obvious intelligence the only thing protecting them. Things were so easy for me and mine, and so very difficult for them.

I knelt down next to the tub. As I looked at my babies

I wondered, how old were little boys when they began demanding protection from their mothers' gaze? It seemed so impossible to imagine. I'd grown him inside of me, created him. These toes I nibbled on, the knees poking up from the water, didn't they belong to me? Isaac dunked his head again, striking out with his legs and catching me in the stomach. The air escaped from my lungs in a rush, making it dramatically clear that this little person was asserting dominion over his own body, that it was separate from me, and belonged to him alone.

"Isaac!" I said. "Watch your feet."

I opened the bath seat and pulled my little round baby out onto a towel in my lap. Sadie was still entirely mine. When I held her it was sometimes hard to remember where I ended and she began. She smiled her huge two-teethed grin and ducked her head, searching for my breast.

"No nursing in the bathroom!" Isaac announced.

"Why not?" I said.

"Just because."

I wrapped my free arm around him to give him some of the attention he resented being directed toward his baby sister, and distracted the baby by kissing the soft folds of her neck. She giggled and wiggled in my lap like a slippery little seal.

"Oh, she's so delicious!" I said, squeezing her fat behind. "Yum!"

Peter said, "I know, she's like a little round cream puff. You want to gobble her up."

"And him, too," I said, pretending to gnaw on Isaac's arm while he giggled.

Peter and I had time to exchange just a few more cannibalistic comments, before I felt a sudden warmth on my lap.

I rose to my feet. "Your little cream puff just peed on me."

Before becoming a mother I would never have imagined how imperturbable I would become, even in the face of bodily effluvia. By now it takes more than a little pee on my clothes to gross me out.

After the kids were safely down for the night, their stories read, Sadie done nursing, Isaac finished with his nightly round-robin of requests—water, pee, water, pee—I stood in my bathrobe in front of my closet. What was appropriate attire for a midnight visit to a neighborhood known for gang violence and prostitution? Does one dress up to interview hookers, or is the casual look more appropriate? I didn't want to stand out too much, but then again I didn't want to be mistaken for a working girl. I decided on jeans and a black sweater, and pulled my hair back into a severe ponytail.

Peter was in his dungeon, sprawled in his desk chair with his feet up on the vaulting horse, his laptop balanced on his lap.

"Where are you going?" he said when I handed him the baby monitor.

"The thing is," I replied, "people like us tend to think the South Side is more dangerous than it really is. We hear 'South Central' and we get all freaked out. But really, what goes on there is primarily drugs and prostitution, and those are victimless crimes."

Peter opened his mouth but I rushed on.

"I know what you're going to say, but I can't bring Al. I have to talk to hookers. Streetwalkers. There's just no way any of them will talk to Al. You know he oozes a cop vibe. He even freaks *you* out, and the worst crime you ever committed was smoking a little pot when you were in college. The hookers will take one look at him and shut down. They're much more likely to talk to me if I'm on my own."

Peter once again tried to speak, but I didn't let him.

"I'll be careful. I won't take any unnecessary risks. I won't even get out of my car unless I have to."

He sat up slowly, his legs dropping to the floor with a thud. "Do you have your cell phone?" he said.

"Of course." On my way out the door I picked up the cell phone I had nearly forgotten. I also shoved a hundred dollars in cash into my pocket, so that I'd have something to hand over if things got ugly.

Eight

On Figueroa Street, cars pulled to the curb, waved down with a flick of a long-nailed hand. The women tottered over on high heels with torn straps, skirts rising up thighs. They ducked their heads into the windows of the cars for a moment and then either slipped inside or stalked away with a toss of false curls. I sat in my car watching this desperate cotillion, partners changing, passed from hand to hand. When confronted with the grim reality, my nonchalance soured. I wasn't exactly afraid. I was anxious. I was, oddly, embarrassed. It took me a long time to work up the nerve to pull my own car forward under the streetlights. When I did, a tall woman with acne-roughened skin and a long red wig leaned into the open car window. When she saw me, the sultry look disappeared from her face like a light being switched off. "I don't do girls," she said, and waved me on.

"I'm looking for someone," I said. "A white girl, Mary something?"

"Do I look like the missing persons bureau?" she said. She banged the roof of my car and moved on to wave down someone else, someone whose needs were more easily assuaged.

Another woman popped her head in. Her face was a Picasso painting of angles, her mouth off-center, one eye bruised and closed shut, the other opened so wide the yellowish white around her iris glowed in the glare of the street lamps.

"What you looking for?" she said. "Forty dollars and you can get whatever you want."

I repeated my request. Did she know Mary? She did not, but she knew of only one white girl who worked that corner. For twenty dollars she'd tell me where to find her.

I sized up the woman's face, her bruises, her disheveled hair, slept on and long uncombed. "I'll give you five," I said. I pulled out the bill and held it in my hand. "Where is she?"

"Up about two blocks, by the taco truck. She'll be there with Baby Richard. She stays by him now."

"Who's Baby Richard?"

"Oh, girl. Everybody knows Baby Richard. He's the little fat man. You can't miss Baby Richard."

I held the bill out toward her and she reached a greedy

hand into the car. "How do I know you're telling me the truth?" I asked.

She snatched the bill and ran clumsily away, limping up the block on one broken heel.

I didn't have a whole lot of faith in my informant, but I also didn't have anywhere else to look. I drove up the block until I spotted a taco truck pulled into a strip mall parking lot. There were half a dozen women leaning against the truck, sipping coffee or eating burritos in quick, greedy bites. Two men sat on the back of a bus bench, their feet up on the seat. Another stood in the lot, yelling up into the face of a blond-haired woman. This man stood no more than five feet tall, but his girth was as much as his height, his vast belly made all the larger by his orange down jacket. It was warm out, probably no less than sixty-five degrees, and he was bundled up as though it were ski season. Baby Richard. It had to be him. And the blonde he was berating was Violetta's friend. She was the only white person there.

I pulled into the lot, took a deep breath, and opened my car door. The eyes of the crowd immediately slid my way, appraising me. One of the men slipped off the bus bench and sauntered away down the street.

"We don't need your condoms or your safe sex lectures, girl. You just get on back in your car and get out of here," Baby Richard said. He was in charge of this parking lot, and he wanted me to know it.

"My name is Juliet Applebaum," I said as I approached. "Violetta Spees's family hired me to find out what happened to her. I'm hoping you might be able to help me."

The round ball of a man stared contemptuously at my proffered hand. I held it out for another few seconds. Finally, he took it. His palm was soft and smooth, a hand unused to manual labor.

"You know who I am?" he said.

"Baby Richard." I turned to his companion. "Are you Violetta's friend, Mary?"

"Mary, Mary, quite contrary," Baby Richard said and laughed loudly. The man remaining on the bus bench laughed, too. The women did not.

"Did you know Violetta Spees?" I asked the blonde.

She glanced over at Baby Richard as if requesting permission to speak. He shrugged.

"Yes," she said. "Violetta and I were friends."

"Would you be willing to talk to me a little about her? I'm not a police officer. I don't work for the government. I work for her sister, and her mother." That was stretching the truth a little; Heavenly had hired us, not Corentine, but I wanted to remind Mary and her keeper that Violetta had a mother who was grieving for her. "We could go get a cup of coffee, or something to eat."

"You all can get a cup of coffee right here," Baby Richard said. He motioned to the truck. He wasn't going to let this girl out of his sight.

"Okay," I said. "Mary? Would you like a cup of coffee?"

"Mary Margaret," she said. "But you can call me M&M. That's what people call me. I mean, out here."

I went up to the taco truck and ordered coffee for

myself and for Mary Margaret. Then I turned to the other women who were standing around staring at us. "Can I buy you all some coffee?" I said.

Ten minutes later everyone was drinking something hot, Baby Richard was busy working on a platter of carnitas, and I was out seventeen dollars. The other women crowded around Mary Margaret and me, pushing their way into our conversation. Most of them had known Violetta. Only one, new to the corner, hadn't met her.

"Were any of you here on the night she was killed?" I asked. "Do you remember seeing her?"

"Of course we was here," a woman in a skintight, purple velour minidress said. "Where we gonna be?"

"Did you see anything? Did you see who Violetta picked up that night?"

The women looked at one another. Mary Margaret looked down at her sandal. She bent down and peeled a flake of gold toenail polish off her big toe.

I said, "Please tell me what you saw. For Violetta's sake. I promise I'm not with the police."

The woman in purple said, "You damn straight you not the police. The police was never here. You think they care about a dead black ho?"

"That's why I'm here," I said. "The police didn't investigate and Violetta's family is looking for some answers. They want justice for her."

"Justice?" one of the other women spat out. "Get real, little girl. You be giving out justice? You?"

"What happened the night Violetta died?" I said, turning to Mary Margaret. "What happened to her?"

A woman who had until now been silently peeling up the rolled paper edge of her coffee cup, spoke up. Her voice was deep and angry and she kicked the ground with one high-booted foot. "Same thing as happened to Niesha, and Teeny, and that other girl, the one with the braids."

"What?" I said.

Mary Margaret said, "Violetta got taken by that man, that same man."

"What man?"

The purple dress woman crumpled her coffee cup in her hand and said, "There's a man been taking girls off Figueroa Street for years. We all know he's here. Every year or so, sometimes every six months, some girl turns up dead. Raped and killed. It's the same man who does it. We know it is. We've known for years."

I felt suddenly cold out there in the dark. "Are you saying there's a serial killer killing prostitutes?"

The woman in the tall boots waggled her head. "You ask yourself, what would the cops be doing if every six months some white girl from Beverly Hills got snatched?"

"I saw him once," Mary Margaret said, her voice low.

"You *saw* him?"

She nodded. "A year, year and a half ago, maybe? The night that girl Teeny got killed. I saw his face. I even talked to him before she did, but he didn't want me." She shuddered. "I saw her get in his car. She never came back out after that ride. Three days later they found her body in a Dumpster."

"Did you tell this to the police?"

She shrugged. "They didn't ask."

"Aren't you afraid to be out here?" I asked her. "He knows you know what he looks like."

Baby Richard smiled, his teeth black with beans. "She don't need to be afraid. She's got me to protect her now, don't you baby?"

"He doesn't take white girls," Mary Margaret said.

Nine

It was too late to call Al that night, and in the morning Ruby and Isaac were buzzing around me like a couple of wasps. I didn't want to talk about any of this in front of them. I was bursting with it by the time I got in to the office.

"You're trying to tell me that there's a serial killer on the loose in Los Angeles?" Al said.

"Yes."

"Juliet, you realize that's crazy, don't you?" He shook his head and returned to his coffee and his files.

"Why? Why is it crazy? Because we haven't heard about it? Because he doesn't have a nickname like the Hillside Strangler or the Night Stalker? We haven't heard about it because he's killing black prostitutes on Figueroa Street and nobody cares." I leaned across Al's desk and covered the document he was looking at with my hand. "Al, those women are scared. They know something is going on. They gave me the names of murder victims." I opened my notebook. "There was a woman named Teeny who was killed about eighteen months ago. And another named Niesha something. They think she was from Compton. She died in 2002. There are others, too."

"Do you know how many murders there are every year on Figueroa Street?"

"No, I don't know how many, and neither do you. Neither does anybody else. Do you know why? Because no one bothers to count them. I'm going to see that Detective Jarin again, and I'm going to tell him about this killer. If that moron had been doing his job in the first place he would have known about these cases. If he'd tried at all, Jarin probably could have found the killer years ago, before the monster even got his hands on Violetta."

I stormed out of the office, furious that Al didn't believe me. I found Jeanelle chopping zucchini with Sadie sitting on the kitchen floor at her feet, stacking Tupperware cups. I plopped myself down next to the baby and pulled her into my lap, bussing the top of her downy-soft head with my lips.

"I'd better take her back up to the city with me," I said to Jeanelle. "I have to go harass a cop and I won't have time to make it back down here before I have to pick Isaac up. He's got an early playdate this afternoon."

"I was going to puree her a little of this," Jeanelle said. "See if she'd eat it."

"She eats anything," I said.

"That is the truth. I had to move the dog dish into the other room when I caught her up to her elbows in the kibble."

"Oh Sadie-sue," I said, snuggling my little girl.

"You and Al have an argument?" Jeanelle asked, her eyes on her long knife as she sliced perfect circles of pale green squash.

"I guess so."

"Oh we did not," Al said. He stood in the doorway, the cordless phone in his hand. "You are one weak-kneed woman if you call that an argument. I've got Robyn on the telephone. She's going to check ViCAP for us."

Al's daughter Robyn was an FBI agent working out of the bureau's office in Houston, Texas. She had inherited her father's love of firearms but, luckily for her, not his looks. She was a beautiful girl, long-limbed and possessed of the kind of confidence that I feared would guarantee her never finding a man. That and the fact that every boyfriend she brought home was given the stink eye and a tour of Al's gun cabinets.

"What's ViCAP?" I said.

"Ask her yourself." Al handed me the phone and I greeted the woman I hadn't talked to since she'd stood guard over my husband and children over a year before.

Robyn said, "Hey Juliet, good to hear your voice."

"Same here. How are things?"

"Good. Good."

I got down to business. "Robyn, what's ViCAP?"

"The Violent Criminal Apprehension Program. It's a system designed to identify serial murders. It synthesizes aspects of homicide investigations from around the country, looking for patterns. It was developed by an ex-chief of police in Los Angeles."

"How does it work?" I asked.

"Police departments send information to NCAVC, the National Center for the Analysis of Violent Crime, located at Quantico. The idea is that if a series of cases is flagged, then the local police departments can coordinate their investigations."

"How do the analysts decide if a serial murderer is at work?"

"They look for similarities of method, of victim, that kind of thing. Some serial killers are so adept at police procedure that they can adjust their methods to thwart the investigation. But the analysts are experts at sifting through the data."

"So if they haven't flagged these murders, then I'm probably wrong? There's no serial killer at work."

"Not necessarily. The system depends on the information it receives. Local law enforcement can't access the system without FBI cooperation, so that makes them less interested in it. Oftentimes, they don't even bother to send us data from their cases, even when they're required to do so. Things definitely slip through the cracks."

"Did your dad tell you about our case?"

"He did. I'll tell you what, I'll run this material and see what we've got for unsolved murders of African-American women in the Southern Los Angeles area. How was your victim killed?"

"Blunt force trauma to the head. He bashed her skull in." I gave Robyn as many details about Violetta and about the other women as I knew. Sadly, what I knew about them was pretty much limited to their race and profession, and to the fact they'd been killed.

"Okay, Juliet. I'll get back to you in a couple of days. Maybe less. I'll see what I can do."

"Thanks." I hung up the phone, and looked up at Al. "And thank you," I said.

"Don't mention it," he said. "Now, do you want to know about your friend Heavenly's criminal record?"

I sighed. "Sure."

"One juvenile arrest under the name Henry Spees, looks like a loitering charge. Referred to diversion and dismissed. Another arrest for lewd and lascivious conduct in a public park. Pled guilty to a misdemeanor. No jail time."

"Men's restroom sweep."

"Yup. Standard stuff. Cops probably found him and another guy doing in public what they should be doing in private."

I shrugged. "So nothing, right?"

"Right. You going over to the 77th Division to bust some heads?"

I stood up, taking Sadie along with me. "No, I'm not

going to bust any heads. I'm just going to calmly and reasonably suggest that Detective Jarin take another look at this case, in light of the statements of the witnesses I interviewed."

CALM and reasonable was a good goal. Calm and reasonable would have been nice. I even started out calm and reasonable, but Detective Jarin's implacable refusal to even consider the possibility that a killer was on the loose turned me shrill and histrionic in record time. I gave him the names of the women who had been killed. I told him about my conversation with the prostitutes at the taco truck. He was unimpressed.

"Look, ma'am," he said. "Do you know how many people get killed in South Central every year? You know how many prostitutes get killed by their pimps or their johns all over this city?"

I'd had this conversation once and I was ready. "No, I don't. Do you? Do you even bother to count the women who get killed? Or do you just chalk it up to an angry john without even spending five minutes investigating?"

"I don't have to listen to this, lady."

We were standing out by the sergeant's desk; this time Jarin wasn't letting me anywhere near the working area of the station. I had Sadie on my hip and was jiggling her while I talked to him.

"Detective Jarin, the women on the streets are terrified. They know this man is out there. They've *seen* him. You have to help them."

"They can't be that scared, or they wouldn't be working the streets every night, would they?" He turned his back on me and walked back down the hall to the door leading into the precinct house.

"Just compare the files!" I shouted after him. "How hard can that be? Just compare them. Look for similarities. Run a few goddamn DNA tests!"

My loud voice frightened Sadie and she burst into tears. As if on cue, I began leaking, large wet circles appearing on the front of my shirt.

"Damn it," I muttered, plucking at my wet shirt. "It's okay, sweetie," I said, trying to soothe Sadie. But she smelled the milk now and nothing was going to calm her but the breast. I looked around the dank waiting room. A few desperate-looking people were slumped on chairs. One older woman stood at the desk, crying and arguing with a uniformed officer. I didn't want to nurse my baby in here, but I realized that neither did I particularly want to be sitting in my car outside on the street in this neighborhood.

"Come on in here, ma'am." I looked over to find the desk sergeant holding a door open for me. "Take the baby in here. I'll watch the door."

"Thank you so much," I said, so relieved my voice cracked.

I followed him into a small room with a metal table and two folding chairs. I sat down and pulled Sadie close. On his way out the door the desk sergeant paused, one hand on the doorknob. "You might want to give Detective Stephen Sherman a call, over in cold cases."

"Who?" I said.

"Steve Sherman. He used to work Robbery Homicide down here. He transferred over to the cold case unit in 2001. He's the man to talk to."

The sergeant closed the door before I could thank him.

Ten

THIS part-time work thing can really wear a person down. Just when you're finally immersed in your work, just when you're making progress, it's time to quit. But I'd promised Isaac a playdate and I had to deliver. I met Isaac's friend Jackson's mom, Sandy, outside the preschool and before we went to sign our kids out we transferred Jackson's booster seat into my car.

"I'm so sorry," Sandy said. "I know the car seat cover smells disgusting. Honestly, I washed it, but I think it's my minivan. It's got this smell. Everything in the car starts to smell like it sooner or later. I think *I* even smell like it."

"Don't worry, I'm sure my minivan's worse. I've tried everything, even one of those horrible little pine trees. I think the only solution is to throw the car away and start from scratch."

"Or we could just give in and market the scents as cologne," Sandy said. "Eau de old yogurt. Sour milk and stale Goldfish body wash."

I liked this Sandy. She had a sense of humor. I also liked her because she looked like she could stand to spend a few hours a week at the gym. She wasn't fat, just a little flabby around the middle. Like me. She looked like a mother is supposed to look, not like the rest of the midriff-baring twig-mommies whose Hannahs and Tylers populated the expensive preschools of the city of Los Angeles. It was such a relief to find someone else who wasn't wearing a skimpy Marc Jacobs top and a pair of size two, two-hundred-dollar jeans. Not that I wouldn't be thrilled to wear a skimpy Marc Jacobs top and a pair of size two jeans, if I could. If I could cram my huge behind into a pair of size two jeans I'd probably own a dozen of them. I'd probably hang a pair on my front door so that everybody, including the UPS driver, could see how tiny I was.

When we got to the classroom Jackson and Isaac were, unfortunately, not speaking. Sandy pulled a note out from Jackson's cubby that informed her that "another child" had hit Jackson over the head with a steamshovel, but that the teachers had put a boo-boo bunny on his lump and he was feeling much better. I had a note in my box that said Isaac had been "having a hard time using his words" and was obliged to come into the classroom while the other children were building a fort in the sandbox.

"Should we cancel the playdate?" I asked Sandy.

She looked stricken. "I have a dentist appointment and then I'm taking Chelsea to her riding lesson."

"Go, we'll be fine," I said.

"Are you sure? I could take him with me . . ." She clearly didn't want to, and I was profoundly relieved that she hadn't suggested hanging out at my house all day to monitor the boys' behavior. I got the feeling that Sandy and I had a lot in common. Jackson was her third child, and I was betting she viewed a playdate at someone else's house like a Get Out of Jail Free card.

"They'll work it out. They always do," I said.

I pushed the feuding nations into their side-by-side booster seats, impressed at the extent of the frost in their relations. Most four-year-olds don't hold grudges this long. Clearly Jackson and Isaac were exceptionally gifted, at least as far as the expression of hostility was concerned. It took two packages of rainbow Goldfish, a couple of juice boxes, and finally, once we got home, hot cocoa with marshmallows before détente took hold.

I put Sadie down for her nap and then went into my bedroom. Peter lay snoring under a mound of pillows and the down comforter.

"Hey!" I said, jumping on the bed. "Hey! It's 1:30. Rise and shine, husband of mine."

He groaned and pushed his head farther under a pillow.

I pulled my socks off and then shoved my feet under the covers, right up to his warm belly.

"Jesus Christ!" he shouted, leaping up. "Popsicle toes!"

"Warm them up, c'mon." I chased him around the bed

with my feet. He grabbed a pillow, stuck it over my feet, and sat on it.

"That is unacceptably brutal, Juliet," he said. "Seriously, can't you think of a more pleasant way to get me out of bed?"

"Like what?"

"Like you could bring me a cup of coffee, or a give me a tender massage."

"Oh please, you'd never get out of bed for coffee or a massage. I could get an air horn. Or dump a cup of water on your head."

"Very funny."

"What time did you come to bed last night?"

He scratched his head vigorously. Like Ruby's, his hair stood up around his head in a cloud of red curls. "I don't know, four-thirty?"

"Well that means you've been asleep for nine hours, buddy. I can't remember the last time I had anywhere near that much sleep. Get your butt out of bed and stop whining." I leaned over to kiss him, to reassure him that I wasn't really bitter about my relative sleep-deprivation. Except of course I was. And he knew it.

"Can you pick up Ruby at school in an hour?" I said. "Isaac's got a playdate, and Sadie's down for her nap. I thought I'd do some laundry and a little research while everything is quiet."

"Sure," Peter said. "Maybe I'll take her to the comic book store. I want to pick up the new issue of *The Escapist*."

"Just keep her away from the big boob comics," I said. When we first had Ruby, I was only too happy to relinquish to her the task of accompanying her father on his comic book runs. Those stores are no fun for the unobsessed. They're not much fun for any woman, frankly. Sure there's always some pierced young girl in there, asking for a copy of *Rurouni Kenshin* or the new *Eightball*, but by and large the denizens are guys like Peter, guys who have wholeheartedly embraced the word "geek." Ruby and Isaac love going with their dad, and as long as they avoid the borderline pornographic books with their drawings of pneumatic-breasted women in spangled leotards, I'm fine with it. Not that I have anything against pneumatic breasts or spangled leotards per se; I just don't want to give either of the kids unrealistic expectations of what their futures hold.

I left Peter to get dressed and started down the hall toward Isaac's bedroom. I had heard nothing from the boys since they were done with their snack, and I feared that silence boded ill. I had no idea how ill, however. They weren't in Isaac's room, and neither were they in Ruby's doing harm to her American Girl dolls. I figured they were probably in the ballroom on bikes or scooters, but I didn't find them there, either. They hadn't tried to sneak into the TV room. I was reluctant to start yelling for them. Sadie was a light sleeper at naptime, and I didn't want to risk waking her. I peeked down into Peter's dungeon; the lights were out and I knew Isaac would rather give up television for the rest of his life than be down there in the dark.

The last room I checked should have been the first. They were in the kitchen. They'd taken a bottle of glass cleaner and a can of Ajax out from under the sink and dumped them in one of my good Italian pottery bowls, then stood up on a chair to reach the bleach on the shelf above the washer in the laundry room, and were in the process of adding the bleach into their concoction.

"Stop it!" I shouted. "Stop it right now!"

Jackson, who was holding the bleach, dropped it on the ground. It splashed over his jeans and sneakers, leaving instantaneous white streaks. I ran across the room, picked up the bottle, closed it, and grabbed the two of them by the arms.

"What do you think you're doing? Are you crazy? Are you trying to kill yourselves?"

The two boys stared at me, at my flaming red face, my wild eyes, and promptly burst into tears. Isaac wailed, "We're just making a blue potion!"

"You can't mix Windex and bleach! They make poison!"

"Poison? Cool!" Jackson said.

I pulled his wet and ruined pants and shoes off him, hauled both boys over to the sink and scrubbed their hands and faces. Then I carried one under each arm and put them out of the kitchen.

"Get Jackson a pair of your pants," I said to Isaac. "And don't you dare leave your room. Jackson, go with Isaac. If you two even poke your noses out of Isaac's room before I say you can, there will be hell to pay."

"But . . ." Isaac began to argue.

"Don't even open your mouth. You're lucky I don't spank you until your tushy turns blue. Go. Now!"

Mopping up the spilled bleach and avoiding ammonia

poisoning wasn't what took time. That I managed in about two minutes. It was the home improvement project that I launched into that ruined my afternoon.

"What are you doing?" Peter said. He was carrying a bleary-eyed Sadie.

"How did you not hear that?" I said.

"I was in the shower, and when I got out I heard Sadie screaming. Juliet, sweetheart? What are you doing?"

I was down on my hands and knees screwing a latch onto the cabinet under the sink. I'd already put a hook and eye on the laundry room door. "Isaac-proofing the house."

"But I thought we decided that those latches would just ruin the kitchen cabinets."

As he spoke a long crack appeared on the inside of the door where I'd turned the screw one too many times.

"Damn it," I said.

"Here, you take Sadie. I'll do it."

I ran carpool that afternoon, leaving Peter with strict instructions. By the time he was done there was no way any child was ever going to open a cabinet or drawer in our kitchen, bathroom, or laundry room ever again. The only problem was that we couldn't open them either.

"You have to push with one hand and pull with the other. At the same time," Peter said, sweat breaking out on his brow as he struggled to open the cutlery drawer. "Ow! I think I broke my finger."

I took his hand and ran it under cold water.

"My mother never baby-proofed our house," he said while we watched his fingernail turn bright red.

"Your mother sent you to the corner store for cigarettes and beer when you were six years old."

He pulled his hand out of the water. I kissed it, and he winced.

"I turned out okay, though, didn't I?"

"Peter, glass cleaner has ammonia in it. When you mix ammonia and bleach you get poison gas. They could have killed themselves."

"Probably not. The room is ventilated."

"Look, do you want to spend the next year sitting by a miniature hospital bed because one of the kids opened the cabinet and swallowed a bottle of lye? Do you want to learn how to clean a little tiny trach tube? Do you want to pick out a miniature casket?"

"Do we even have lye in the house? Why would we keep lye in the house?"

"Peter!"

"Okay, okay." He put his arm around me. "We'll figure out how to use the latches."

I rested my head against his chest. "I can't believe it. What am I going to tell Sandy when she comes to pick Jackson up? Thank God it wasn't one of those other moms. They'd never let their kids come over ever again."

Peter kissed the top of my head. "Honey?" he said.

"What?"

"Why do we have lye in the house?"

"We don't have lye in the house," I said, pressing my face into the soft cotton of his shirt. "Who would keep lye in the house? I don't think I even know what lye is."

Eleven

ROBYN called the next afternoon. "I've got about eleven possible cases," she said.

"Eleven?" I replied, aghast.

"I only went back to 1998, and I limited myself to unsolved rape-murders of African-American women. As near as I can tell, all these bodies were discovered in the thirty-block Figueroa Street corridor. I can't be sure I got them all, because that area's pretty much the most violent part of the city. The murder rate went way down in the nineties, but there were still lots of files for the computer to sift through. These eleven stuck out for me, though, because they're all African-American women, all most likely prostitutes or at least women who the investigating officers assumed were prostitutes. There's only one thing that bothers me."

"What's that?"

"Your victim was bludgeoned, right? A blow to the head?"

"Yes."

"Well, most of these others are strangulation cases—eight to be exact. The other three of the victims died from other causes; there's one other woman who was beaten to death, like your victim. Two others were stabbed."

I leaned back against the kitchen counter. I was holding a large knife in my hand, my biggest and sharpest blade. Ruby, Isaac, and I were making cookies, and we were just getting ready to cut up a tube of premade dough into little triangles. I looked at the sharp steel.

"Hey guys," I said. "Go ahead and use your fingers."

I carefully put the knife back in the drawer and closed it. The latch clicked into place. I moved to the other side of the kitchen, away from the children's prying ears.

"So, Robyn, does this mean the cases are connected or they're not?"

"I don't know. Like I said, perpetrators are known to change methods. I'd like to turn all this information over to the NCAVC team."

"Please do," I said. "Maybe they'll light a fire under the cops' behinds."

"The LAPD isn't going to be happy, and I'm not sure the NCAVC team will think it's worth pursuing, but I think it's worth a look. Something feels wrong to me here."

"Thanks, Robyn."

"I'm happy to help. Oh, Juliet. There's one other thing."

"What?"

"I found three cases in the late nineties that look a lot like the others. You know, African-American prostitutes who worked Figueroa Street. These were strangulation cases, too."

"So why didn't you include them in the list?"

"They're not unsolved cases. One man pled guilty to all three murders. Vernon Smith. He's been in jail since 1998."

"Oh." I know that the logical conclusion from Robyn's statement is that those three crimes are different, the work of that incarcerated man, and that the ones since then were done by other people, or one other person. But, I had spent years as a criminal defense attorney, and I still think like one.

"What was the basis for the conviction?" I said.

"There was a guilty plea, but I can't tell more than that. I don't know if there was a confession or if there was other evidence. The cases were closed out after the defendant was apprehended." She paused. "They sure do look just like all the others, though. At least like those eight other strangulations. They look just the same."

THE next morning I took Robyn's list of names and went to look up Detective Steve Sherman, formerly of the Robbery and Homicide Division, currently of the cold case unit. A man less like Detective Jarin I could not have found.

Detective Sherman was a big man, bald but for a circlet of grizzled hair running around the back of his head from temple to temple. He wore a pinstripe suit with wide lapels and slightly flared pants, a suit that looked exactly like the latest in men's fashion. I couldn't see Detective Sherman combing through the racks at Barney's or Fred Segal, however. He'd been wearing that suit since the last time it was in style, circa 1977.

Before we sat down Detective Sherman wiped out a mug with a paper towel and poured me a cup of coffee. I thanked him and took a sip. I couldn't keep from grimacing.

"Sorry," he said. "The other guys all go to Starbucks, so I'm the only one who drinks it. I forget that other people don't like it so bitter."

"It's fine," I said. "I need the caffeine." I pulled Robyn's e-mail with the list of victims out of my bag. When Detective Sherman had returned my call he'd been eager to see me. Surprisingly eager, in fact.

I pointed out the three solved cases. "I know you've got these listed as solved, but I left them on because they're so similar to the others on my list."

He shook his head. "I know those cases. There was a confession."

"Confessions can be coerced."

He sighed and scanned the rest of the names on the list. He tapped a name with his finger. "This was mine," he said.

I looked at the name. Lanelle Walcott, murdered on February 11, 1999.

He said, "I've been thinking about Lanelle for a long time. Sometimes, you know, they just stick around in your head." He passed his finger along her name, gently, almost a caress. "She had twin baby boys. Same age as my grandson."

"What happened to them?"

He shrugged. "The grandmother was sick with diabetes; she'd lost her leg and wasn't in any shape to take care of them. They went into foster care. I hope they were adopted."

He knew as well as I did that the fate of a pair of African-American twin boys in foster care was not likely to include adoption.

"Did you have any physical evidence in that case? Anything for a DNA test?"

"We had a autopsy. Real complete," he said. "We had semen, blood. The works."

"Did you do DNA testing?"

"Back then? No."

"And now?"

He motioned at the pile of folders on his desk. "You know how many cases we've got in this unit?"

I shook my head.

"Nine thousand. Nine thousand unsolved homicides, going back to the 1960s. And the crime lab has a two-hundred-case backlog. We can't do DNA testing on every case."

"Why not?" I said. "We can afford to incarcerate two

million people in this country, most of them on nonviolent drug offenses. Why can't we afford to do DNA testing on all the unsolved murders if we've got something to test?"

He just shook his head. "They're doing their best over at the lab. We're all doing our best."

I leaned forward, my elbows on his desk. "I know you are. I know you're all doing your best. But it's not good enough, Detective Sherman. Not when all these women are dead. Not when the ones who are alive face the possibility of being raped and murdered every time they set foot on Figueroa Street."

He picked up Robyn's e-mail and scanned the list again. "Can I keep this?" he said.

"Yes. I've got a copy at home."

Twelve

It was a week before I became frustrated enough to come up with a plan. A week in which I wrote up a case report to Heavenly that contained only my own suspicions and the fears of the prostitutes. A week in which I under-billed my hours. (One more piece of paperwork to hide from Jeanelle.) A week in which I tried to get two different newspaper reporters to write an article about the murders. One man wouldn't even return my call. The other, a young metro section reporter, took all the women's names and told me he would look into it once he finished the long series he was doing on illegal gambling among teenagers.

Over the course of that week I found our last Arthur Fanswatler, the assistant manager of a Club Med in the

Caribbean. Our movie studio client was happy, and we would get paid.

At the end of the week, over an Ethiopian lunch at a place called Café Blue Nile—a restaurant that Al and I were sampling in order to determine if the beg wat melted in our mouths and the doro tibs fell off the bone like at our old favorite, the Jewel of the Nile, recently closed by the health department—I leaned back in my basket chair, my fingers covered in lentils and my mouth burning from a dozen kinds of hot peppers, and said, "This is driving me out of my mind."

"I know," Al said. "I think the sauces are better here, but the meat is too tough. It's a hard call."

"Not this." I waved at the platter covered in dollops of mushy stew, which we were eating with our fingers and with the help of pieces torn from the huge soft pancake on which the food sat. "This is great, although you're right about the lamb. It's too stringy, or something. I'm talking about the Spees case. It's been over six months since she was murdered."

Al licked his fingers clean and drank half his water in one gulp. "Man that's hot. Yeah, it's been six months."

"The women I talked to said he hits every year, sometimes every six months."

"You're worried he's going to kill someone?" Finally, by dint of sheer tenacity and repetition, I'd won Al over to my point of view. He was at least willing to accept the possibility that there was a killer out there. Especially since it appeared that Robyn agreed with me.

"Yes, I'm worried that he's going to kill someone. I'm also thinking it's a perfect time to try to find him."

"What are you talking about?"

"Look, what would the homicide cops be doing right about now if they were actually investigating the case?"

Around a mouthful of food, Al said, "DNA testing the samples."

"I mean in addition to that."

"Why don't you tell me, since you're suddenly such an expert on police procedure."

"They would do a stakeout! They would send a plain-clothes officer onto Figueroa Street dressed as a hooker, to try to lure the killer out of hiding."

Al sighed and wiped his face with his napkin. "Maybe on *Starsky & Hutch* they'd send out a decoy, but not at the LAPD. You think they'd risk a cop's life?"

"Sure, I mean, don't they do that kind of stuff all the time?"

"You've been watching too much television, my dear."

"Al," I said. "We've got to help these women. What if while we're sitting around waiting for Robyn to convince someone at the FBI to look at this, or for the LAPD crime lab to get through its backlog, the guy decides to strike again?"

"What are you suggesting, that we dress you up as a hooker and send you on the street? You've got three kids, Juliet. Don't be an idiot."

"I could never do it."

"Well thank goodness for that."

"He doesn't like white women."

Al pushed his basket chair out from the table. It creaked and snapped under his weight. "What are you planning? Please tell me you're not planning on calling Robyn and asking her to be your decoy."

"I thought of that, but she'd never go for it. Even if we found him she'd lose her job."

"I wouldn't let her, anyway."

I ignored his blustering. "There's a much simpler way. You and I can stake it out. We give the hookers my cell phone number, and if they see him they call us. We'll call the cops and, you know, pin the guy down until they get there."

"Pin him down?"

"Not physically. You'll pull your gun on him."

"And if *he's* got a gun?"

"He doesn't. If he had a gun he'd have used it by now. He strangles them or he beats them over the head. This guy likes to use his hands."

Al rubbed his face, and in the dim light of the restaurant I saw the back of his hands, gnarled and scarred, with gray hairs sprouting from the knuckles. The hands of an old man. Al was so vigorous, so tough and strong, that I often forgot that he was not a young man. My first year at the federal defender's office we celebrated his fiftieth birthday with cake and a stripper, that bit of inappropriate conduct courtesy of his fellow investigators. I counted on my fingers. He was fifty-eight.

"There's a big flaw in your plan," Al said.

"I know. How would we know when he's going to hit?

It could be tonight, it could be six months from now. We can't sit out there every single night, and it won't do the girls any good if we're not right there when it happens. He and his victim would be long gone by the time we showed up."

"Yeah, that's a flaw, although I was thinking of another one."

"What?"

"I was thinking that it's an insane idea and you're a friggin' lunatic."

I wish I could say that it worked, that Al and I did a stakeout, one of our usuals, complete with In-N-Out burgers, Krispy Kremes, and not too much to drink. (When you're on a stakeout, you can't leave the car to go to the bathroom and, while Al swears that adult diapers are a tried-and-true technique of investigators the world over, peeing in my pants just doesn't appeal to me.) I wish we had been the ones who busted the guy. But a stakeout was a ridiculous idea. It was doomed to failure. Anyone could see that.

Which is why we only went out once, that following Wednesday. I chose that night because Violetta was murdered on a Wednesday, as were four of the victims on the list. And because it took me that long to browbeat Al into coming along and to convince Peter that I wasn't going to get killed.

We pulled up at the taco stand at 9 P.M., long before I expected that anything would happen. The girls knew me by now, and they came right over.

"You buying tonight, girl?" The woman who had been wearing the purple dress the other night now had on a little sequined number, silver. Over her hips and breasts where the fabric tugged the sequins had popped off, leaving dangling white threads.

I pulled out some cash and bought a round of coffees for everyone. I got played a little—half the girls wanted some Mexican pastries, the others put their burritos on my tab—but I didn't mind. Once the young couple in the truck had served us, the woman replying to my *buenas noches* with a shy smile tucked behind her palm, I told the girls my plan.

"How we going to call you?"

"Do any of you have cell phones?"

Mary Margaret and two of the other girls had them.

"How we going to know it's him?"

I said, "M&M, can you describe him?"

She shrugged. "He's just, you know, a guy. Real short hair. He's good looking, you know? Not like you'd think." She considered her shoes. "Um, he's a black guy, did I say that?"

I don't know why I was surprised. I guess I had always just assumed he was white. The classic serial killer is almost always a white man. "Are you sure?" I asked her.

"The guy I seen Teeny with was black," she said. "No doubt. And we'd know a white guy right away, you know? He'd stick out driving up and down Figueroa."

"You don't get white tricks?"

"Sure we do," she said. "Just, you know, we notice them."

Not for the first time I wondered how it was that Mary Margaret had found herself working this corner. What in her life had led her here? Was it drugs that precipitated the fall, or did drugs just make it easier to bear once it happened?

I gave the women my number and pointed to Al's Suburban. "I'll be in that car, okay?" I said. "We're going to drive the corridor, park on a side street. If anything happens you just call. Or flag us down."

The woman in the sequined dress said, "Don't go getting yourself shot, okay? Watch where you're parking that car, and if anyone bothers you, you just tell them that Baby Richard's girls said you could be there."

"Thanks," I said.

For the next five hours Al and I drove the corridor slowly, always keeping the blocks between Eighty-fourth and Figueroa and the taco truck no more than a couple of minutes away. We parked on side streets, we pulled into parking lots. We stayed on one dark block with a good line of sight for over an hour, until the porch light of the house we were parked in front of went on, and an angry woman wearing a head full of pink curlers pushed aside her curtain and glared at us. We watched the girls get in and out of cars, drive away, come back. They were never gone for very long. Finally, at two A.M. I said, "This is stupid. He could come out any night. Any night of the year."

"No kidding."

"Let's go home."

Al pulled the car up to the corner and I jumped out. Mary Margaret was just coming out from behind a car.

She had a compact mirror open and was putting on lipstick.

"We're going to call it a night," I said. "You've got my number. Use it if you need to. Call me if anything happens, if you see the guy, anything."

"Yeah, okay," she said, but I didn't have much confidence that she'd call. As far as she was concerned I was just one more impotent person, one more person who had failed to protect the girls on Figueroa Street.

Thirteen

EARLY the next week, Detective Steve Sherman called me. I was in my kitchen, trying to pry open a drawer. A measuring cup had rolled up under the baby latch and jammed it.

"Can I trust you?" the detective said.

"Trust me to do what?" The blade of my knife snapped off in the drawer, and I stumbled backward.

"Goddamnit," I muttered.

"Can I trust you to keep your mouth shut?"

I felt a wrenching in my stomach, anxiety twisted up with hope. I dropped the knife handle on the counter. "Yes, you can trust me. What happened?"

"You'd be surprised at how many of those old cases had some kind of bodily fluid evidence."

"Yes? And?"

"I sent five samples to be tested. I walked them over to the crime lab myself and asked them to do DNA testing ASAP."

"You said there was a backlog."

"Yeah, but you know what? Sometimes a little friendliness can move mountains. The phrase serial killer can do that, too."

"You got a match, didn't you?"

"Yup, four of the five matched. One of them was one of the three closed cases."

"The rest of the women on the list were all killed later than those three closed cases."

"Right."

"So that means the guy who confessed couldn't have killed them."

"Vernon Smith. Yes, it looks that way. I pulled the other two cases he pled to. I've got a blood sample from one, and I've got semen and fingernail scrapings from the third. I sent those in for DNA analysis. If they come back a match then we're looking at a DNA exoneration for Mr. Smith."

"So you have an innocent man in jail, and a murderer out on the street who killed at least four women, maybe more. Jesus Christ. You've got to run that DNA sample against your database."

He didn't say anything.

"Oh my God," I said. "You already did that. You ran the DNA sample against the general database. You got a hit."

"If this leaks, it's as much as my job is worth."

"Please tell me."

He was silent for a moment. "Look, you're the reason I looked into these cases in the first place. But if you go to the papers, or if you tell the victims' families before brass authorizes, then I'm up a creek."

"Please, just tell me."

"We got a live match. Guy name of Charles D. Towne struck a plea on an attempted rape and gave a DNA sample as part of his sentence. It's him. He's good for these four murders, and who knows how many others. We're testing DNA from every open sex murder we've had in the past fifteen years."

"Maybe you shouldn't limit yourself to the open ones."

"If those other two cases Vernon Smith pled to match Charles Towne's DNA, then Vernon will go free, I give you my word. I will move heaven and earth to get Vernon out of jail."

"Oh thank God," I said. "When can I tell Violetta's family?"

He paused. "Violetta Spees?" he said.

"Yes, Violetta Spees. That's the woman whose family I'm working for. I told you that."

"That's the one that didn't pop."

"What?"

"We had a decent semen sample from her, more than enough to test, and it showed up different. Charles Towne didn't kill her."

I felt the floor fall away under my feet. I sat down heavily on a kitchen stool. "Could there be some mistake?" I said. "Could you have accidentally tested a sample from someone else? What if she'd had sex with more than one person that night? She was a prostitute, maybe there was someone else's DNA there, too."

"We found just the one. And there are other things about the Spees case. Things that make it different from the others. She was killed with a blow to the head. The other four, all of them, were raped and strangled. They had much more bruising and tearing. When they autopsied your victim, they did a toluidine stain and there wasn't any damage."

"What's that? What's a tolu . . . ?"

"Toluidine stain. The medical examiner swabs a blue stain to the entire perineum to see if the skin is damaged or abraded. It only shows up blue if there's injury."

"And in Violetta's case?"

"No blue."

I couldn't imagine what I was going to tell Heavenly. We had found a serial killer but we were no closer to finding her sister's killer than we were before I had begun looking for him.

"Juliet," Detective Sherman said. "I can't make the case officer on Violetta's case do anything, and I can't officially do anything until she ends up in the cold case unit, but I owe you. You need anything, anything at all, you come to me, okay?"

Cold comfort.

"Thank you. Thanks, Detective Sherman. And thanks for taking me seriously. When are you going to go public with all this?"

"We're notifying the victims' families today, and the prosecutors are putting together the charges on the first four cases. We hope to be able to issue a press release by this afternoon."

Fourteen

I couldn't bear the idea of Heavenly hearing the local news and rejoicing, even for a moment, in the belief that Violetta's murderer had been found. I broke my word to the detective. I felt terrible about it, but I would have felt worse if I hadn't. I did it in person, not on the phone.

Heavenly worked in the back office of a bustling orthodontics practice in Beverly Hills. I waited for her in a large room decorated top to bottom with an astronomy theme. Morose children with mouths full of sapphire blue and violet braces sat kicking their heels against couches upholstered with astrological signs. A boy strapped into medieval-looking headgear stood before a mural of the planets, complaining to his mother that Jupiter was too big; it was all out of proportion. Heavenly came out to get me and was greeted cheerfully by the mothers, one of whom asked after an insurance claim.

"Don't you worry, Lucy," Heavenly said. "They'll pay. Sooner or later they get so sick of hearing my voice on the phone that they put the check in the mail."

The woman smiled with obvious relief.

Heavenly told me that she was in charge of all the billing, not just for these four doctors, but for half a dozen other practices as well.

"I started out as a medical receptionist," she said, showing me to a large office full of computer equipment and file cabinets. "Within a year they had me doing billing. Pretty soon I realized that I could streamline the whole system and take on additional clients. I've got a nice deal worked out here. I'm employed by this office, so I get a good benefits package, and office space for me and my two clerks, but then I do outside work, which I charge other doctors for directly. It's worked out real well, so far, and we're going on five years."

"That's terrific, Heavenly. It really is." I was going to have to reconsider the discount I gave her.

She made room for me on a low chair, piling a few files and a large stuffed bear onto a credenza pushed up against the wall. "Isn't that the silliest thing?" she said, pointing to the purple bear. "One of the dental supply reps gave that to me last Easter. He's got a crush on me, don't you know."

"I've got some hard news, Heavenly."

Her smile faded.

I told her about Charles D. Towne and about the DNA

test that showed he hadn't been Violetta's killer. She grew very still, her manicured fingers resting lightly on her desktop, the tip of her red tongue just visible behind her slightly open lips.

"They caught this man?" she said. "He's under arrest?"

"Yes. They're notifying the families of the victims right now, which is why we're not even supposed to know anything about it yet. But they'll go public later today or tomorrow. It's all still confidential, but the cold case detective who solved the case let me know what was going on. I couldn't let you hear about it on the local news."

"How many girls did this man kill?"

"Four for sure, but they're testing other cases. I gave Detective Sherman eleven names, in addition to Violetta's. And there are others. Lots of others."

Air hissed through her nose. "He killed more than eleven women?"

"He killed a lot of women. I don't know how many. We'll probably never know how many, unless he confesses."

"All those women, disappearing off the street, getting raped and murdered, and nobody cared. Nobody cared at all."

Tears gathered on the tips of her eyelashes, and she tilted her head back, dabbing at the corners of her eyes with her index fingers, protecting her makeup just like she had the last time I saw her cry.

"I'm not finished with this case, Heavenly," I said. "Violetta was someone's victim, even if she wasn't Charles Towne's. If you'll allow me to, I'd like to keep looking. I haven't even begun to investigate old boyfriends, friends. That pimp Baby Richard, maybe he had something to do with it."

Her eyes focused on mine. "You want to keep on?" she said.

"Yes."

"Okay, you keep on. You keep on. I want to know who killed my sister. My mother deserves to know that the man who did this will be punished. Violetta's child deserves that."

Fifteen

WHEN Sadie sleeps, she rolls onto her belly and sticks her little butt up in the air. She reminds me of a turtle, with a humped middle and dainty little feet poking out. I stood in the open doorway of her room, my eyes slowly growing used to the dark. The yellow of the hallway light faded to orange as it crept into her room, bathing her small body in a faint glow. I stilled my breath so I could hear the muffled rumble of hers.

"Hey," Peter whispered, coming up behind me. He slid his arms around my waist and rested his chin on my shoulder. "Sweet, isn't she?"

"Yes."

While we watched, her budded mouth pursed and her tongue clicked against the roof of her mouth. She was dreaming of nursing, I thought. She was dreaming of me.

"Should I turn her over?" I asked in a low voice.

"Why? You'll just wake her up."

"She's not supposed to sleep on her stomach. She's supposed to be on her back."

At every appointment with the pediatrician for the first few months of Sadie's life we were reminded to never, ever, put her down on her stomach, that if we did we would lose her to too deep a sleep, a sleep in which she stopped the rumbling breath that was at once so clear and alive, and yet so tenuous. They don't tell you what to do when the baby begins rolling over by herself, flipping from that splayed and awkward turtle-on-its-back pose to this more natural-looking one.

"If she's strong enough to turn herself over, she won't stop breathing," Peter said. "Anyway, aren't we beyond the SIDS age?"

"It could still happen," I whispered. "Anything can happen."

Peter turned me gently away from the doorway and closed the door quietly behind us. We walked down the hall past the bedroom where Isaac sang to himself in the dark, and the room where Ruby lay, wide awake, staring at the ceiling, or sneaking a book under the covers with the flashlight I left on her bedside table, knowing she would do this, remembering myself at her age. She was plagued by the same insomnia I had suffered as a child, and my memories of it were too vivid to do what my mother did. I would never lurk outside my daughter's bedroom door waiting to hear the rifling of pages so that I could catch her in the act.

We lay side by side on the living room couch, the couch I chose expressly for this purpose, so that my whole family could loll around on it.

"What's going on with you?" my husband said. He was winding a lock of my hair around his finger, making a sausage curl.

"What do you mean?"

"You're not acting like yourself. Sadie's been rolling over onto her stomach since she was four months old. You've never once even considered flipping her back."

"Yes I have. I think of it every time I see her on her tummy. The first thing I think of when I see her like that is that her risk of SIDS is doubled."

"Do you really?" he said doubtfully.

I sat up, crossed my legs and stared at him. "Don't you?"

"No."

"Are you trying to tell me that when you wake up before she does in the morning, you don't immediately think that she died in the night?"

He shook his head. "No. I mean, I almost never wake up before her, but I wouldn't think that even if I did."

"Not even when she was a newborn? Or how about Ruby, before we knew anything at all about babies? Don't you remember the first night she slept through the night? We woke up at five in the morning and were positive she was dead. We even agreed you should go get her because I wouldn't have been able to stand seeing her body." I shuddered.

Peter folded his arms behind his head and gave me a look that seemed far too akin to pity. "I remember you woke me up and told me to check on her. I remember how freaked out *you* were. I didn't come to the same conclusion. It's just not the way I think. I don't know, maybe it's a maternal thing."

"Okay, well how about this. What's your first thought when Isaac is late coming home from a playdate, if he's being driven home by another kid's mom? What's your immediate explanation for their delay?"

Peter shrugged. "I don't know, that they hit traffic or something."

"You see, I immediately assume that they had an accident, and that the car seat she used for Isaac was an old one, and it didn't work, and that he's lying in a puddle of blood on the 405."

Peter sat up and took my hands in his. "Juliet, sweetie. That's insane. You realize you're a crazy person, right?"

"I can't help it. I see this incredibly dangerous world, full of all these possible disasters, and I'm terrified. Even by things I know are crazy. I know that Ruby isn't going to be snatched by a pedophile; I know that the chances of that are exactly zero. But when I see those big Amber Alert signs on the freeway I get this sick feeling in the pit of my stomach. I see her name and description up in those lights, with the description of some nightmare killer's car, and, like, half a license plate number or something. Not enough for the cops to trace . . ."

"Stop it," he said. "Don't you realize you've taken this

fantasy way too far? You've worked out the details. That's just . . . I don't know. Insane. It's insane."

I fell forward onto his chest. "I know. I know it's insane. It's worse now, because of Violetta, and that evil Charles Towne."

"But he didn't kill Violetta. Charles Towne had nothing to do with Violetta's murder."

I sat up again and said, "Right. That's exactly the thing. There's some other horrible killer out there. Some other guy smashing women's heads in. That makes it all so much worse. It's not just one serial killer who got caught because he was too stupid to use a condom. Who knows how many there are lurking out there?"

"Juliet, now you're talking like one of those neurotic, crazy mothers. Like that one who wanted to LoJack her kid. That's not you."

"But it is. It *is* me. I'm just like that LoJack nut. I *am* a LoJack nut! I'm just as worried that something terrible will happen to one of them as she is. I'm just as worried that Isaac will drink bleach, or get hit by a car, or that Ruby will get leukemia, or that they'll become retarded from mercury poisoning because they eat canned tuna. I'm terrified that Sadie will fall off her changing table and hit her neck at just the right angle to paralyze her for the rest of her life. I'm just as crazy as the rest of the moms—the only difference is that I do a better job of faking it. I do such a good job that I even convince myself."

I collapsed again, and waited until I felt his arms around me. He didn't say anything, and then, softly, almost inaudibly, he murmured into my hair, "Maybe you need a new job."

I sat up. "Don't be ridiculous," I said. "I love my job. I love working with Al, and I love investigative work. Plus, what else could I do for only three or four hours a day? I couldn't go back to being a lawyer."

In a voice so tentative it was clear that even he knew this idea wasn't going to fly, he said, "You could just be with the kids."

I thought of the confidence with which I'd left the Federal Public Defender's Office when Ruby was a baby, how sure I'd been that staying home, being a full-time mom, was not just what was right for my daughter, but what was right for me. I thought of the hours of playing Candy Land, walking to the park, pushing her on the swing. I had been unprepared for how slowly the time would creep along, how interminable a day would feel. I'd been unprepared for how lonely and bored I would be.

But I'd also been unprepared for the intensity of my passion for my children, how their lives would consume and subsume my own, just as their bodies had irrevocably altered mine. The physical self that looks back at me from the mirror is a perfect metaphor for how they have altered my entire life. My breasts, about which I used to be so proud, now pointed south, nipples stretched, elongated beyond all recognition by three voracious mouths. My belly, once smooth and firm, rounded, yes, but with unmarked milky skin, now hung, a loose and crepey expanse, striped with shiny silver lines. It requires an elaborate origami just to button my pants, and when I take off my bra, I swear I can polish the tops of my shoes. They've done the same to my life, these three. I used to run from courthouse to jail, from oral argument to crime-scene investigation, my whole focus on my clients, those poor men for whom mine was the only voice. With Peter I *played.* We went out to dinner, we saw movies, we spent long languid evenings talking about ourselves, about each other, about the world. But once the babies came, they filled every space. Not just their needs, manifold though those are. It's their breath, their presence. They fill my field of vision from end to end. There's so little recognizable now, either of my physical self or my old life.

It's difficult to figure out how to move them aside, even just a little, to make a small nook for myself. Even those few hours a day, hours in which I have Sadie with me as often as not, give me something. They give me the chance to look outward, beyond them and me. They broaden my focus just enough to keep me from going out of my mind.

"I can't quit my job," I said.

"Then maybe you have to figure out a way not to take it so much to heart. Not to let the fears infect the rest of your life."

Peter knew as well as I did how impossible that would be for me. One of my worst failings as a public defender was that I got too wrapped up in my cases, in my clients. Against them was levied the enormous power of the government—police, prosecutors, even judges. The United States versus one lone man. I couldn't let them face that all by themselves, so I threw myself into defending them. Sometimes I worried that a cooler head, a less invested one, might have done the job better. I had victories, I won cases, but I also made enemies of the prosecutors, railing against what I saw as their imposition of injustice. I even got thrown out of the courtroom once. The only reason the judge didn't hold me in contempt was because I was ten days away from my due date and looked like a whiskey barrel with feet.

"I'll try," I said, nestling my head against Peter's chest.

"Okay."

"That's all I can promise."

"You know, Juliet. The world is a lot safer a place than you think it is."

"No it isn't," I said. "You're just foolishly optimistic, that's your problem."

"Maybe you're foolishly pessimistic, have you ever considered that?"

"I'm a realist."

He sighed and kissed the top of my head.

Sixteen

AL, Chiki, and I stood staring at the white board on which I'd written a list of every possible suspect, likely or unlikely, in Violetta's murder. It was a depressingly short list, and at the same time nearly infinite. I'd divided the list into categories, and the very first, the category in which we were most likely to find the murderer, I called Tricks. Under that, in a different color pen, I'd written Unknown. Under Boyfriends I had three names. The first was Deiondré. Then there was Vashon's father—I'd connected that one to the Tricks category with a dotted line. The final one was Baby Richard. I put a red question mark after Baby Richard's name, because, after all, I didn't know if Violetta had had a romantic relationship with him. I didn't even know if she worked for him or for another pimp.

I had a category titled Family, because it never makes sense to ignore the family of a murder victim. I'd written everybody's name in that column, including Vashon, Tamika, and Monisha, just for the sake of completeness.

We stared at the board for a minute, and then I said, "Wait a second," and added another category: Coworkers.

"Coworkers?" Al said, doubtfully.

I wrote in Mary Margaret's name, and "Purple Dress Hooker." I left room for other names as I learned them.

The three of us continued to stare at the board.

Chiki said, "I like how you used different colors. That's just what I was hoping you'd do when I bought that multipack of dry erase markers. It looks real organized."

"Thanks," I said.

We stared some more.

"Don't expect me to go making rainbow charts of *my* cases," Al said.

"Nobody expects that," I said.

"Although it would probably organize your thinking," Chiki said. "The color coding can be real helpful. Like the way I tagged the different folders on your computer desktop. You like that, don't you?"

"Don't touch the computer, Chiki," I said, for perhaps the thousandth time. As one of the conditions of his supervised release, Chiki was barred from all contact with computers. However, getting his hands away from a keyboard was harder than getting Ruby and Isaac to stop bickering. They might not do it in front of you, but as soon as your back was turned, they were right back at it. Al and I had been trying to get this supervised release condition lifted so that Chiki could do his job, or even move on to one that made better use of his proficiency at writing and deciphering computer code, but the probation department and the court were unwilling to listen to reason. How they expected a person to survive, let alone find work, in this day and age without computer access, was beyond me.

"Where are you going to start?" Al asked me after we'd had plenty of time both to appreciate my arts and crafts project and to assimilate the true hopelessness of our task.

"Deiondré, Baby Richard, and the hookers," I said. "At least I know who they are."

Seventeen

BACK I went to the Thurgood Marshall projects. Before I paid a visit to Deiondré, I stopped by Corentine's house. I'd picked up a few little presents for the kids—a couple of young adult novels for Tamika, two kissing teddy bears for Monisha, and a *Vote or Die* T-shirt for Vashon. They were at school, of course, but I gave the things to Corentine, along with the lemon meringue pie I'd bought from Al and Janelle's neighbor, Millie, a sweet old lady who supplemented her pension and social security checks by baking for her friends. I had a standing order with her for a pie every week, and although I knew Peter would be furious that I'd given away dessert—especially on an evening when we were expecting company—I didn't like to come by Corentine's house empty-handed.

"Oh, how lovely, Juliet," Corentine said. "Did you bake this yourself?"

It would have been nice to take the credit for having slaved away in the kitchen, but not even I could lie so blatantly. "No, I'm afraid I wouldn't even know how to begin to bake a pie."

"I could teach you. It's easy as pie!" She laughed at her own joke. "Come on in. We'll have us some coffee and a slice of this beautiful pie."

She poured two cups of coffee, added a dollop of mocha-flavored nondairy creamer and two teaspoons of sugar to each, and handed mine over along with a thick wedge of the trembling yellow and white pie.

"Mm," I said, taking a bite.

"It's good," she said. "I do mine on a graham cracker crust, but this is nice, too. Bad for my sugars, but nice."

"Your sugars?"

"I have the diabetes."

"Oh no! And I brought pie."

"Don't you worry. Alls I need to do is test my sugars and see if I need to fix my medicines a little. It's nothing."

I let the meringue dissolve on my tongue. Corentine Spees was an easy woman to be quiet with. There was something both soft and grounded about her presence. She neither demanded nor expected to be entertained with conversation; it was enough to share a companionable cup of sweet coffee and listen to the click of our forks on the plate. When we were done I picked up the plates and brought them to the sink.

"Oh, you don't have to do that," she said. "You're a guest in this house."

"I like to help," I said.

Corentine heaved herself up from her chair. When she was sitting her bulk seemed to settle, a kind of immutable mass. As soon as she was standing she became light on her feet. She moved quickly, her fingers darting through the contents of a box she took down from above the fridge.

"Let me show you some pictures of Violetta. She came to Sunday dinner the week before she died, and Heavenly had just bought herself a digital camera. She took all these pictures and then she printed them out in her office. Just like that. Didn't have to pay for them or nothing." Corentine found an envelope embossed with the name of Heavenly's orthodonist employers. She pulled out a small stack of photographs. "I know there's at least a couple with Violetta in them." As she leafed through them she smiled. "Look at that Monisha being silly with her auntie's shoes."

Monisha was caught midstride, tottering on a pair of long silver sandals. Violetta had big feet, not that much smaller than the sister who had started out a man.

Corentine said, "Here's Violetta, but it's a bad one. Look at her behind her boy."

Violetta sat on the sofa, with her hand extended in front of her face toward the camera, and her body bent as if trying to duck behind the boy who sat next to her. Only the creased palm of her hand and the backs of her long fingers tipped with pointed nails were in focus. Vashon, however was facing the camera, his mouth open in a wide grin, laughter pushing his cheekbones so high they turned his eyes into merry slits. The glee in his face was palpable enough to melt the paper the photograph was printed on.

That was the first time the case made me cry. I looked at Violetta's little boy sitting next to his mother, full of joy, breathless with excitement at the feel of her body next to his, and my eyes filled.

"He loved her so much, that poor child," Corentine said. "He just loved her like the daisies love the sun."

It was the perfect simile. When I saw this boy his face was closed, a knot of pain and anger. Here, he was like a flower blossoming, open and easy.

"This is a good picture of Violetta." Corentine handed me a photograph of Violetta and Chantelle. They sat at the table next to each other, each wearing an identical and practiced smile on her perfect rosebud of a mouth. Violetta's hair was done up in braids with long, ragged extensions. Her eyes were smaller and set deeper than her sister's. The most striking contrast between the two was their skin. Chantelle's was like smooth satin, rich and bright under the hanging lamp. Violetta's face was pitted, her color flat as though it had a wash of gray over it. A raw-looking scar, bright pink against her skin, lifted up her right eyebrow. She looked much older than Chantelle, much older than her twenty-four years.

Corentine stroked the photograph with her finger. "She looks tired in this picture. That night I put her to work mashing potatoes, just like you did when you come to dinner. She said to me right out, 'Mama, I tired. I so, so tired.' She told me she wanted to go to sleep in her old room and sleep for a hundred years. She said, 'I'm a sleep and wake up a whole new person.' "

"Did she stay that night?"

Corentine stuck out her lower jaw and sucked her upper lip into her mouth. She knotted her brow. Then she shook her head. "God help me, I put her out. I put her out into that dark night."

With a full-throated wail, she collapsed, heavy as stone, into my arms. I staggered backward; she must have weighed over two hundred pounds, far too much for me. It took all my strength to lower her into her chair. She beat her fists on the table. I hugged her and she wrapped her massive arms around my waist. We were like that for a long time, long enough for me to grow conscious of the weight of her pulling at my hips. Finally, she took a dish towel off the table and blew her nose into it.

"Oh Lord, look at me. Crying like a baby. I can't even imagine what Heavenly would say, she saw me like this with you."

"It's all right," I said. "You've probably been so busy being strong for the children that you haven't had a chance to let yourself just have a good cry."

"I'm just going to go fix my face," she said. A few moments later she was back, her lips colored mauve, her eyes red but dry.

"Corentine," I said tentatively. "Would you tell me what you meant when you said you put her out? Did she ask if she could stay?"

She nodded. "She just come to dinner that day, knocked on the door at four o'clock. Before that it was two months since I seen her. She would call on that cell phone Heavenly gave her, but she didn't come over for two months. Then she just walked in so easy. Like she been coming every week."

"How often did she call?"

"Sometimes every night, sometimes not for weeks. She forgot all about us when she was on that crack, or when she was shooting the heroin. She liked to talk to Vashon when she been drinking, though, and if she didn't sound too bad I'd give him the phone. He'd tell her all about his teachers and his homework. I'd have to take the phone away if she got to crying, because that made him real sad."

"Was she on anything when she came that Sunday night?"

"No, she was clean. She told me she been clean for two days. But Thomas, that's Chantelle's husband—you didn't meet him because he was working the night you come over. Thomas, he brought some beer and she drank some of that. She didn't get drunk, just happy and silly at first, and then all sad, like she does. She asked me could she come home. First I said 'Yes, of course you can. You know you can always come home.' But then she drank another of Thomas's beers, and she started looking drunk, all off her feet. She got silly with Ronnie, and I said, 'That's it.

You can't be in my house and be drinking and using drugs. You get on out now.' And that's the last time I saw her. That's the last time I saw my baby." She started crying again, tears running over her plump cheeks and pooling in the creases of her neck.

"What do you mean, she got silly with Ronnie?"

Corentine pressed her mouth into a thin line. "Just silly. Drunk silly. Wasn't nothing, but I didn't like it. Not in my house."

Try as I did, I could not get her to define the word silly with more particularity. It was obvious that it made her too uncomfortable. She got up and started bustling around the kitchen, washing the dishes we'd dirtied with our treat. I could tell she was finished talking, that she felt she'd said too much already.

Eighteen

My visit to Deiondré was far less emotional than my hour with Corentine. I found him sitting on the front steps of his town house, smoking a cigarette and drinking a tall can of malt liquor. He held his cigarette with his thumb and forefinger, the way I remember boys doing when we were in junior high school, hanging out behind Friendly's and doing our best to look cool while we coughed up lungs full of mentholated smoke. Deiondré had a shaved head and a pronounced ridge across the top of his skull, as though the plates of his skull had not closed quite right when he was a baby, but instead had overlapped each other.

"Deiondré?" I said.

"That's me."

"Do you mind if I have a seat?" I said, motioning to the steps where he sat.

He gave me a look of exaggerated surprise, and then shrugged and shifted over. His legs splayed out in front of him, knees spread wide and bright white sneakers lolling.

I sat down, trying not to make a face at the stream of cigarette smoke he blew in my direction. The steps were wide, and I could put about two feet of space between us. I said, "So, Ronnie Spees said you'd talk to me about his sister."

"Ronnie said that?"

More or less. "Yup," I said. "I'm a private investigator and Heavenly hired me to find out who killed Violetta."

He laughed. "You a private investigator? You one a Charlie's angels?"

"I like to think of myself as more of a Jim Rockford kind of girl."

"Who?"

"Never mind. What can you tell me about Violetta?"

He blew a smoke ring and then a straight stream right through it. "Henry Spees, he hired you?"

"You mean Heavenly, yes she did."

"Heavenly," he snorted with disgust. "I ain't calling Henry Spees nothin' but Henry Spees no matter how big his titties is."

I turned slightly so I could see him. His thick neck was circled by a yellow-gold chain. The choker was so tight it wrinkled the skin above and below it. "So, Deiondré, Violetta went home with you the night of her son's birthday party, right?"

"No," he said, shaking his head at the very idea. "No, I ain't take that nasty ho to my mom's house. You crazy or something?"

"But you were with her that night?"

"I took her out in my car. That Violetta, she thought she was something, when all she was was a ho who'd do anything for a rock. Hell, she'd do pretty much anything for a forty!" He tipped his can at me and then took another gulp, smacking his lips loudly.

"What did you do with her?"

"I ain't telling you."

"Did you have sex with her?"

"I didn't have sex with Violetta!" he said, making his voice prissy and high-pitched, in unfair imitation of mine. "She did her business, and like I said, I gave her a rock. We had us a transactional relationship." He laughed loudly, and took another slug of his malt liquor. "A transactional relationship," he said again, very pleased with himself for coming up with the phrase.

"Was that night your only transaction?"

He shrugged. "Sometimes she'd call me. You know, 'Deiondré, come take me out.' If I had nothing better to do, I'd take her for a ride in my car."

"Engage in another transaction?"

He cackled. "Now you know it, baby."

"Did you see her the night she died?"

"What, you think I killed that ho? Please, I wouldn't waste a bullet out my gun. Last time I saw her she was running out her mama's house, all up in my face. 'Deiondré, let me stay with you. Deiondré, take me somewheres.' "

He shook his head. "Like I ever gonna let that ho in my house."

"Was that the Sunday before she died?"

"I don't know. It was a couple days later I heard she was dead. My moms, she went to the funeral and all."

"Did you go to the funeral?"

"Nah," he said, as if the very idea was absurd.

"Did you do what she asked that night? Did you take her somewhere? For a ride in your car?"

"No. I had my baby's mama coming over that night. I didn't need to go for no ride with no messed-up ho."

Deiondré knew none of Violetta's friends or clients, or at least would not admit to knowing any. He knew nothing of what happened to her after he wouldn't let her inside his mother's house that Wednesday before she died. After a while, he grew sick of my questions and said, "You want to come inside? You old, but you look pretty good. I wouldn't let Violetta inside my house, but you can come right in if you want."

"Thank you, Deiondré," I said, getting to my feet. "It's a tempting offer, but I'm afraid I'll have to say no."

"Suit yourself," he said, and lit another cigarette off the butt hanging from his lip.

Nineteen

THAT night all I wanted to do was mull over the case, but instead, I had to host a dinner party. This was the first real grown-up affair Peter and I had put on in our house in the months we'd been there, and as little as I wanted to, I had to stop thinking about the case and be charming to my friends. I had found a replacement pie for the one I'd given to Corentine, also lemon meringue, but far too perfectly formed to pass as homemade. Peter wasn't fooled, but neither was he annoyed with me for giving away our pie. He'd been raised by his mother, after all, who subscribed to the notion that you shouldn't show up anywhere empty-handed. Her idea of a hostess gift might be a Jell-O mold, a twenty-four-pack of Yodels, or a bottle of Night Train, but the principle was the same.

Our guests this evening were my friends Stacey and Kat, and their families. These were people in front of whom we were not ashamed to fail, should our attempts at California cuisine be derailed by the reality of life with three children and a very old stove. Stacey is my oldest and closest friend; we've known each other since our freshman year of college. For most of our lives we'd engaged in a bare-knuckled competition, but a few years ago I'd had to concede defeat. Stacey is a partner in a major Hollywood talent agency. She makes more money in a month than I do in a year, more even than I did when I was working full-time at the federal defender's office. She makes so much money, in fact, that she has started engaging in the ultimate of cash-wasting hobbies—she has a contemporary art collection. This is a woman who wrote her freshman art history final paper on the place of Salvatore Ferragamo in the twentieth-century aesthetic. Back then I had doubted her, saying that unless Pablo Picasso and Henri Matisse donned Ferragamo slippers in their studios the shoemaker was not likely to have been a particularly significant influence, but she'd gotten an A on the paper. My thoroughly researched and highly original analysis of the works of the surrealist Leonora Carrington earned a B+. Shows what I know.

Now Stacey is amassing one of Los Angeles's finest private collections of American collagists. Everyone needs a hobby.

Stacey's son Zachary is a few years older than Ruby and has always been frighteningly precocious. That night, while Peter rushed around the kitchen scraping drippings into gravy boats and chopping vegetables for the salad, Stacey stood in his way, reading aloud from an essay Zachary had written on the long-term repercussions of the national deficit on the capacity of United States to engage in international borrowing.

"I want an unbiased, professional opinion," she was saying. "Is it crazy to think the *Los Angeles Times* would publish an op-ed piece by a ten-year-old?"

"I don't know, Stace," Peter said. "That's not really the kind of writing I do."

"I *know* it's not the kind of writing you do, I'm just trying to decide whether the writing is good enough to send off for publication."

Peter began pulling the drumsticks off the three chickens he'd roasted. Our oven might not cook evenly, but it sure could cook a lot of food.

Kat wrinkled her forehead. "I didn't understand a word of it, Stacey," she said. "Which probably means it's erudite enough for the *Times*." Kat and I met in prenatal yoga classes. She had found this house for us after much Sturm and Drang, including the murder of one of the occupants of the first house we'd wanted to buy. Having me as a client was probably one of the reasons that Kat decided to quit the real estate business to stay home with her kids.

Kat's baby, Azure, was a delicate and fine-featured little thing, slender and graceful even as a six-month-old. She had miniature hands and feet, large round eyes, and a mass of dark curls. Next to her, Sadie looked like a German weight lifter.

"Are you sure I can't help with something?" Kat said.

"Peter hates when people try to help in the kitchen," Stacey said. "He doesn't even like it when Juliet tries to."

Peter said, "I don't object to Juliet's help on *principle.* It's just that she's totally incompetent and more likely to do permanent damage to the kitchen than get the dinner on the table."

"That's so unfair," I said. "I'll have you know I know how to make mashed potatoes."

"But I'm not like Juliet, Peter. I'm a good cook," Kat said.

"*Your* help I object to on principle," Peter said as he sliced the chicken.

"Why?" she said.

Stacey rolled her eyes. She'd heard this before.

Peter wiped his hands on his red-and-white checked apron. He said, "Here's the thing: I don't want you to help in *my* kitchen, because when I go to your house, I don't want to help in yours. I just want to sit around and be waited on."

"Are you sure you're not Iranian?" Kat asked.

"Very funny," her husband, Reza, said. He had just wandered in from a protracted tour of the house led by Ruby and Isaac. "I saw your office, Peter. It's quite something."

"It's definitely something," I said. "We're just not sure what."

Peter accepted assistance in ferrying the meal to the dining room and we all sat down at the heavy oak table. Even with ten chairs and two highchairs, the room didn't seem crowded. It was long and narrow, running the entire length of the house. Like the other rooms it had wrought-iron sconces, although the ones in here weren't gargoyles. They were meant to look like candles, complete with dripping wax and flickering flames.

While we were serving ourselves from the heaping platters, Andy, Stacey's husband, said, "I'm hoping I'll be able to hit you up for a new public interest project my firm's pro bono office has gotten involved in."

"What's that?" Peter said doubtfully. Andy is a corporate lawyer. It was hard to imagine him prying himself away from a hostile takeover to file 501(c)3 papers for a public interest organization.

"Hoops for Humanity," he said. "It runs basketball programs in low income neighborhoods. The idea is to give the kids something to do so they're not out on the street dealing drugs and robbing people."

"Basketball players rob people?" Isaac asked.

"No," Ruby said. "That's the point. Basketball players don't rob people. Right, Andy?"

"Exactly," Andy said.

"It's not really quite the point," I said. When I was a public defender, Andy was one of the people who always asked me how I could possibly live with myself for defending "that kind of person." I couldn't even shut him up by pointing out that, as far as harm to humanity goes, my note-drop bank robbers hurt far fewer people, even if you consider the bank's investors and depositors, than Andy's take-over clients. My clients had never brought down entire banking and business conglomerates, causing the unemployment of thousands and the bankrupting of pension programs. That argument never made much headway with Andy. He's one of those guys who thinks that the Enron management team shouldn't have been penalized for seeing an opportunity and exploiting it.

I said, "I think the basketball programs are designed to protect kids, to give them a place to go. I think it's more of a question of providing a mentoring system, opportunities for positive social interactions, that kind of thing."

"There's where you're wrong," Andy said. "It's an investment program. Invest a few dollars on balls and courts and keep the criminal element busy. The good kids are already doing their homework in the library every afternoon; they don't need basketball. This program is great because it targets the really dangerous ones, the ones we want shooting hoops instead of preying on us and our families."

Every time Andy has an affair with some twenty-two-year-old I cross my fingers and hope that this is the time Stacey will finally cut him loose. They've been separated and reconciled more times than I can count. They even filed for divorce once. It never fails; he promises to change, she lets him move back in, and he plays at devoted husband and father for just long enough to ease her suspicions. Then, as inevitably as cockroaches return to a New York apartment after the exterminator's come and gone, Andy goes back to his old ways. I can't stand the man. I really can't.

"Why are they dangerous, Mama?" Isaac said.

"Because they shoot people," Ashkon, Kat's older son, said. He's Isaac's age, and they share a fascination with things like guns, shooting, and death. "They shoot people with machine guns and pistols."

"All right, enough is enough," I said. "*They* do not shoot people, whoever they are. Andy, I don't want to get into a long sociological discussion about the prevalence of violence in the inner city, and the struggles of inner-city children faced with a country that views their color as enough reason to cross to the other side of the street and deny them basic rights like a clean place to live. Or about a government that spends ten times more incarcerating children than it ever bothered to spend educating them."

"At some point even victims need to take responsibility for their own behavior," Andy said, sanctimoniously.

The thing is, I *agreed* with him. I agree that the culture of victimization exploits the victim as much or more than the victimizer, and that individual responsibility is important. I agree that a basketball program is a terrific idea, even if all it's designed to do is keep kids busy so they have no time to jack cars. But what always amazes me about the people who make these arguments, people like Andy, is that they assume that if the positions were reversed, if they were living not in Brentwood McMansions but in the Thurgood Marshall projects, if they were forced to study in a school with no funds for art programs, Advanced Placement classes, or even textbooks, if their parents were serving twenty-year sentences for nonviolent drug offenses, they would be one of the good kids. They always assume that they would be working in the public library after school, studying for their college entrance exams and avoiding the seduction of the street. They always assume that they would successfully pull themselves up by their bootstraps and excel. Nobody ever imagines that he would be one of the ones who couldn't hack it, one of the ones who would fall prey to the easy oblivion of the crack pipe, one of the ones who would decide that there are easier ways to pay your mother's rent and buy your baby's Pampers than to work at McDonald's for six bucks an hour.

"It sounds like a great program," I said, biting my tongue. "We'd love to support it."

"Great," Andy said. "I'll put you guys down for two tickets to the first gala fund-raiser. Unless you want to take a whole table? Depending on where you sit, it's either ten or twenty thousand dollars for a table."

"Andy, don't be ridiculous. They'll sit at our table," Stacey said.

"Can we be excused?" Ruby said.

"Sure," I said, happy enough to get her and the others away from the all-too-adult conversation.

"Can we put on a video?" she asked.

"Try to find something else to do," Peter said. "You've got a whole posse of kids here. Play explorers or something."

"There's nothing to explore!" Ruby said. "We know every place. Can't we please just watch a movie?"

Peter said, "Zachary and Ashkon don't know all the secret places in the house. I'm sure you guys can figure out something to do. We'll call you when it's time for dessert."

Ruby looked appealingly at me, as if seeking review from the bench. I just shook my head and waved the four children out of the room. "Show them the attic," I said. "Just be careful with the ladder."

"Is it very high?" Kat asked. "Are you sure they'll be all right?"

"It's fine," I said. "It's one of those pull-down things. It's more like a set of steps than a ladder."

"Maybe they should pile pillows at the base of it, in case someone stumbles," Kat said. "Ashkon!" she called after the children. "Ruby! Make sure you pad the floor under the ladder with something." She turned back to me. "I'm not sure the attic is such a good idea. Ashkon's a little nervous about heights."

"I'll tell them to keep to the main floors," Peter said, getting up and following the children. When he came back he asked our guests, "Did you guys see the stories in the paper about the serial killer they caught?"

"What a horror," Stacey said. "I just can't believe this could be happening a few miles from us, and we heard nothing about it. It's terrible."

"Juliet was the one who pointed out that the murders were connected," Peter said. He told the story of my search for Violetta's murder.

"That's amazing," Kat said. "I'm so impressed with you."

Stacey said, "You were driving around at night in South Central Los Angeles, by yourself? Are you insane?"

"Al was with me most of the time."

"Oh, Al, well that makes me feel better," she said sarcastically. "Is his car bulletproof? Was he providing protective cover with an assault rifle?"

I stood up and started stacking our dirty plates. "It's not as dangerous as you think."

"Sweetie, they found a serial killer. And the maniac who killed your client is still out there. Of course it's dangerous."

I knew Stacey was just concerned about me. I knew, too, that she was right. But I still resented what she said.

"My client isn't Violetta. My client is her sister, and by extension the rest of the family. They've gotten no help from the police, and they're living in a special kind of hell knowing that the man who killed Violetta is still at large. They deserve to have someone on their side."

Stacey caught my wrist in her hand, "Hey, I know they do. And they're lucky to have someone as tenacious as you, but please be careful, okay? Give me your word that you won't do anything stupid."

"You'll never find the guy who killed her," Andy said. "It's probably just another lunatic. The city is lousy with them."

"Well, I have to try," I said. As I carried the dishes into the kitchen I wondered if Stacey had noticed that I hadn't promised anything.

Twenty

I worked from home the next day, which I tried to do at least a couple of days a week. It limited my actual productive time to naps and car trips, but it was sometimes better than driving all the way down to Westminster. It also allowed me to multitask, or as Peter says, do many things badly at the same time, which is what I was doing when Heavenly returned my call. I picked up the phone while I pulled a crumpled silk T-shirt out of the dryer. I flipped over the tag and read, *Dry Clean Only*.

"I was calling to find out what happened between Ronnie and Violetta at Sunday dinner the week before she was killed," I said. I had debated calling Ronnie and asking him directly, but I wasn't sure I'd get a straight answer from him. Heavenly was more likely to tell the truth, I hoped.

There was silence on the other end of the line.

"Heavenly?"

"What are you talking about?" she said.

"Your mother told me that she told Violetta to leave because she got drunk and was acting silly with Ronnie. What does your mother mean by acting silly?"

"She said that? She said Violetta was acting silly with Ronnie?"

"Yes, she did," I said. I lugged the overflowing laundry basket into the dining room where I had a nice large expanse to fold on.

"Look," Heavenly said. "You know my sister was not a perfect person. She had a lot of problems that she just could not control. She couldn't control herself when she drank, and she sure couldn't control herself when she used drugs."

"I know, Heavenly, and I'm not trying to condemn her. I'm just trying to get an idea of what was going on with her right before she died. You know, get a fix on her emotional state."

"How is hearing all this ugly family stuff going to help you find her killer?"

I paused, the phone tucked up under my chin, a half-folded sweatshirt in my hands. Could Heavenly really not imagine the answer to that question?

I had not underestimated her.

She said, "Ronnie had nothing to do with Violetta's death. The very idea is crazy. I'm not paying you to make up stories about my brother."

"I'm not saying he did. You're paying me to turn up what information I can, and the only way I know how to do that is to ask a lot of questions."

Heavenly remained silent for a few moments. Then she said, "I'm going to tell you what happened, but only because I'm sure it means nothing."

"I'm sure you're right."

"My mother doesn't keep alcohol in the house, but poor Thomas had been on duty for something like two days straight, and he was exhausted and stressed out. He brought a six-pack, maybe two. Violetta was fine before he and Chantelle came. She was playing with Vashon, she looked at his homework and his report card. She even did Monisha's hair. When Ronnie came, she was sweet as sugar with him, just like a big sister, asking about his girlfriends and his classes. But when Thomas showed up with that beer, well, Violetta just got to work on it. You could see Mama getting more and more upset; she took it real hard when Violetta was like that. Violetta barely touched her food. Mama made a gumbo and Violetta just picked at it, all the while drinking her beers. After dinner, Ronnie and the children put on a video. Violetta started talking about how there was no room on the couch for her. Then she sat down in Ronnie's lap. Next thing we know he was jumping up, and she was lying on the floor hollering. Mama came rushing from the kitchen yelling at him that he hurt his sister, and Ronnie said Violetta was touching him."

"Touching him like . . ."

"Touching him like a sister has no business touching her brother."

I was holding a pair of Isaac's pants in one hand, and Ruby's T-shirt in the other. Now I dropped them on the table. "Had anything like that ever happened before?" I asked.

"With Ronnie? No." There was a meaningful silence on the other end of the phone.

"With someone else? One of your other brothers?"

"Walter's been in jail for nearly ten years. Marcel's only been gone for three, but I can't imagine he would have stood for that."

"With who, then?"

She didn't speak.

"With you?"

"Years ago, she was staying at my apartment. I used to let her stay there a lot, when she was tired of being out on the street. I was usually smart; I'd lock up my purse and my jewelry. But one night, I had a date and it didn't go so well. I came home really upset and I drew myself a hot bath. I took my earrings and necklace off and left them out on my dresser. I soaked in the bathtub for a good long time, and when I came out I saw she'd taken the earrings and the necklace, too. They were a matched set, twenty-four karat gold, with little ruby chips. I loved those, and she knew it. They were the first real jewelry I ever bought for myself. Violetta came home about four in the morning, her arms all shot up. She'd traded my jewelry for heroin."

My laundry lay in an unfolded pile, and I sat down, unable to do anything but listen.

Heavenly continued, "I started yelling, cussing her out. And she tried to tell me I was too stressed out, and then she offered . . . well, she offered to relieve my stress."

"She tried to have sex with you?"

"I was a woman, living as a woman and all that, but it was before my final surgery. She offered to. Well. You know. With her mouth."

"Oh. Wow. What did you do?"

"What did I do? What do you think I did? I threw her out. I was never much of a man, but I am a big, strong, powerful woman, and I just picked her up and tossed her right out on her ass."

"When did you see her again after that? Things must have been incredibly difficult and awkward between you."

"You know what? I don't think she even remembered it. Next time I saw her was at my mother's house maybe a month or so later. She acted like it had never happened. So I did the same thing. I never told anyone about it until just this minute."

"Do you think she remembered but pretended that she didn't?"

"I have no idea. Only the Lord knows what went on in my sister Violetta's head."

In our country, we like our victims to be pure. Children, innocents, those are the kinds of victims for whom we can work up compassion. Once we have anointed a victim, once we have verified her blamelessness and determined that she is worthy of our regard, our devotion to her memory and her cause burns with a white-hot intensity, at least until we are distracted by another equally pure casualty of misery. We rallied around children with AIDS, boys like Ryan White because we decided their diagnoses were a result of disease not behavior. But we could never bear to lend our support to the cause of gay men who caught the disease in the bathhouse or the bedroom. In describing the AIDS crisis, our newspapers actually used the words "innocent victims," words that specifically excluded gay men and women like Annette Spees, whose death came at the hands of a dirty hypodermic needle. The same is true when a woman is raped. We demand that she be virginal, or at least modestly pure. We scrabble through her sexual history like squirrels foraging for nuts, searching for the evidence of promiscuity that will absolve our seven-foot basketball player or our group of rollicking fraternity boys. Only the rapes of innocents are free of this rapacious gossip-mongering.

I swore I would not be like this. I would not be like the police officers who ignored Violetta's murder, led a perfunctory investigation, kept a file almost symbolic in its thinness, and then filed it away after a few brief months. I would not value Violetta's life any less because she was a drug addict who sold sex so casually that she could thoughtlessly offer it to her own brothers. I swore that, like her family, I would cherish Violetta. I would fight against the pointlessness of her death more than she had fought for the quality of her own life.

As a public defender I represented the people society pushed aside, those who had been cast out as a threat and danger. It had come easily to me to see each of my clients as a person capable of affection, of transcending his crime and his criminality. Yes, my clients were almost always guilty, and some were guilty of heinous crimes, but without exception they touched my heart. There was the man guilty of a series of take-over bank robberies—armed with assault weapons he had stormed a bank, firing bullets over the heads of the tellers, emptying their drawers. He had once had a wife and son, and he took great interest in the baby I was carrying; he asked me every time we met how I was feeling, he pulled my chair out with shackled hands, and in the middle of his trial, leaned over and told me he thought I looked pale and should ask for a short break to rest. Another client remembered my due date from prison and sent a meticulously handcrafted card, a colored-pencil drawing of a clown holding a handful of balloons in the shape of letters, spelling out the words *Welcome Ruby*. Other clients asked me to check on their mothers, to make sure they were safe and healthy. Becoming a mother myself did not cause me to fear these men more. On the contrary, when Ruby was born I seemed to grow even more open, more able to realize that there was something to value in everyone, some light behind the dark of their eyes.

After I hung up the phone with Heavenly I made a pact with myself. I would serve Violetta's memory in honor of that principle of fundamental human good. I would not let myself forget that Violetta's son loved her so much that his smile burst the confines of his face, or that she loved him enough to try to go straight, again and again.

I thought of all those clients I had, and then, inevitably, I thought of Charles Towne. If it had fallen to me to represent him, would I have found any humanity in him? I don't mean charm; I know that they're often charming, these sociopathic serial killers. I am not asking whether his facile charisma would have succeeded in causing me to forget his crimes. I am asking whether I would have been able to see beyond his hideous deeds to something else within. I don't know. I don't even know if such a person possesses a fundamental humanity, or if these particular criminals, the Ted Bundys and the Charles Townes, if they alone of all I've stumbled across are hollow, nothing behind their eyes but the horror of their desires.

Twenty-one

It was easier to pull a rap sheet on Baby Richard than you might have expected, given that I had no idea what his real name was. Al didn't even have to call in a favor from a friend in Vice. We found Baby Richard on the web. Or, rather, Chiki found him on the web. Not that he was using the computer. Of course he wasn't, because that would have violated the conditions of his supervised release.

Let's just say *someone* found Baby Richard. Someone pulled up a site that listed the credits to a documentary on HBO, a documentary on the lives of pimps. That same someone went to the video store, and watched this hour-long documentary and found not just Baby Richard's name, but a thirty-second clip of him walking up the red carpet to some kind of pimps' ball, wearing a purple hat with an ostrich feather and a matching full-length purple fur coat. A subtitle flashed with the name "Joaquin 'Baby Richard' St. Pierre."

"His name can't possibly be Joaquin St. Pierre," I said. "Why would anyone named Joaquin St. Pierre be called Baby Richard?"

"I ran it," Chiki said. He handed me a faxed printout. Joaquin St. Pierre had a pimping and pandering arrest record dating back more than ten years. There was one assault arrest on his record that had not resulted in a conviction, and a few minor drug possession raps, one of which had landed him sixty days in county.

"It must be him," I said. "Man, how the mighty have fallen. From a pimps' ball in a purple fur coat to a taco truck on Figueroa Street."

"You go where the business is," Chiki said. "If he's running enough Figueroa Street girls he's probably taking home more money than you are."

"That's hardly saying much," Al said from across the room. Jeanelle had gone over the billable hours last night, and she had not been happy. Al and I split the expenses for the agency, and we each took home what was left of our hourly rate. It didn't really cost him when my billables were down, but it made Jeanelle tense. She wanted to see the business in her garage earning some real money, probably because she wanted us to get the hell out of there and into an office of our own. Although why she imagined we'd ever leave now that the garage came with free childcare, I don't know.

"I don't get the whole pimp thing," I said. "I know they supposedly bail the women out of jail and provide protection, but it still seems like the women are getting a seriously bum deal. These guys," I waved at the television set. "They're walking around in sequins and plumes, driving Bentleys, for God's sake. Violetta barely earned enough to keep herself in dope, and M&M doesn't look like she's bought a new pair of shoes in years. And it's not like the pimps are doing such a great job of protecting the women. Baby Richard and the rest of them didn't keep the prostitutes on the corridor from getting picked off like fish in a barrel. Why don't the women just team up and do for each other what the pimps are supposedly doing for them? They could have, like, a cooperative."

"Hey, Norma Rae," Al said. "You going to go talk to this guy tonight, or what?"

I shrugged. "I guess so. Although what am I going to ask? 'Hey, Baby Richard, do you mind telling me if you killed Violetta? Did you bang her across the head because she wasn't earning, or was it something else?' "

That's not exactly what I said, although what I came up with was hardly less ridiculous. That night I found him in his usual place, by the taco truck.

"What you doing?" he called out when I pulled into the lot. "Running some kind a free meal program?" Baby Richard thought his jokes were far funnier than other people did. Now he leaned over, wheezing with laughter, slapping the side of one of his thick thighs.

There were half a dozen women standing in the parking lot, and they rushed over to me as soon as I got out of my car. My old friend was back in her purple dress and this time she wrapped me in her arms and pulled my face right into the fabric. Her dress was rough against my cheek, and she smelled so strongly of a musky, sharp perfume that my nose ached.

"You did good," she said when she finally let me go.

The other women pressed in closer, nodding. "We know they caught that man because of you," another said.

"I didn't do anything," I said. "It was that cop in cold cases who did it all. And you all. You're responsible for catching the guy far more than I am. I just told the cop what you said. He was the one who sent the cases over for DNA testing and found the match."

"We know you made them do it," the woman in the purple dress said. "We know that if you hadn't come they wouldn't have looked at what happened to Teeny. It took a rich white woman to start shouting before they would do anything. We know that, and we're grateful to you."

"Thank you," I said, finally. I felt uncomfortable taking credit for having solved the series of murders. All I had done, after all, was ask someone to look. But she was right, of course. It took someone who looked like me to make the cops open their eyes.

"The thing is," I said, "Charles Towne didn't kill Violetta. There was no DNA match for her, and she was bludgeoned, hit in the head. I'm still looking for the man who killed her."

The women looked surprised, and then one of them shrugged. "Probably just a crazy trick," she said. They nodded and began to drift away, back to the taco truck, the dingy, white sun around which their world revolved.

I bought my usual round. By this time even the men hanging out with Baby Richard expected a free cup of coffee. M&M walked up just as I was paying. She pulled a roll of bills out of her bra and handed them to Baby Richard. Out of the corner of my eye I watched him lick his fat thumb and count the bills, ostentatiously slowly. When he was done he raised an eyebrow.

"That's all," she said.

He didn't speak, just frowned.

"He didn't want anything else."

"Your job is to make him want it," he said. He added the money to the thick wad he pulled out of his pocket. Then he reached one arm around M&M and brought her close to him. His head reached no higher than her neck. He ducked his chin and kissed her gently on the swell of one breast. "You know how to do that, don't you, baby?" he said. Then he bit her.

"Ow!" she screamed and pulled away. She swatted at his face with one of her hands and he easily ducked away from the blow. "Goddamnit," she said. "You hurt me!"

He laughed and high-fived one of his buddies.

"Look at this," she shrieked pulling away the collar of her shirt. "You left a mark. You marked me!"

"You damn right I marked you," he said. "Next time you going do what you know you need to, or I'll mark you more than that."

She ran across the parking lot, tottering on her spiky heels. When she reached the taco truck I handed her a cup of milky, sugared coffee and a sweet roll. She took the food, sniffling.

I turned to Baby Richard. If I wasn't afraid of him before, I was now. The casual glee he took in hurting M&M made my skin crawl, and made me fear that hurting me would cause him no less pleasure. My mouth felt dry and I took a long sip from the cup of coffee I had kept for myself. Then I walked over to the bus bench where he had resumed his seat.

"Baby Richard," I said. "You wouldn't mind talking to me for a few minutes, would you?"

He laughed his trademark high-pitched wheeze. "Sure thing. Come on and sit right by Baby Richard." He shifted over on the bench, patting the seat next to him. I glanced at his thick thighs spreading across the seat.

"I'm fine right here," I said.

He shrugged and laughed again. Then he waved the other two men away. They glided off in the direction of the women.

"What can I do for you?" he said.

"It's about Violetta," I said.

"What the hell else is new?"

"Excuse me?"

"That what you always come here to talk about."

"Did Violetta work for you?" I asked.

"What you mean, did she work for me?"

"Was she one of your girls?"

"Was she one of your girls?" He mimicked me in a whiney falsetto so much like the one Deiondré had used that I was forced to confront the possibility that that was the way I really sounded. Then he laughed again, slapping his thighs with both hands.

I waited for his amusement to abate. "Was she?" I asked. "Her friend M&M is. I was wondering if she was, too."

He looked me up and down, his eyebrow cocked as it had been when he was counting M&M's earnings. Then he shrugged. "No," he said. "She wasn't one a mine."

I tried to figure out if he was telling the truth.

"With a ho like Violetta," Baby Richard continued, "you just don't know what she going to do. She as like to shoot her money into her arm as give it where it belongs. She's *unreliable*. I do not tolerate unreliability."

"Are you saying you don't let your girls use?"

He laughed his wheezy laugh. Clearly Baby Richard found me endlessly amusing. "Girl, every one of these hos use. What you think get them through they days? You think you be able to do what they do without a rock in a pipe or a needle in your arm?"

I stared at him, astonished at the perception he showed, and at his indifference to his role in all of it. "So why was Violetta different? Why wouldn't you have wanted her?"

"Why you think my girls with me?" he asked, leaning back on the bench.

"I don't know," I said. "Protection?"

He shook his head in disgust. "Girl, you straight trippin'. It's love. L-O-V-E. Every one a them loves me. They like to take care of me." He held his hand out to me and I saw a wide ring set with a glittering diamond shoved onto his fat pinkie finger. The stone could not have been real; it would have been five or six carats if it were. But it sparkled, reflecting the light of the streetlamp. "They see me rollin' with the bling, and they be proud. They love me, you understand?"

"They love you," I repeated trying to keep the doubt from my voice. "And Violetta didn't love you?"

"Violetta didn't love nothing but the drugs. I can't work with a girl who don't love nothing."

She loved her son, I thought. At least a little bit. Not enough, though. Clearly not enough.

"You go back to Eighty-fourth Street," he said. "You see a man sitting in a ugly old Chevy, white with red interior. That's Violetta's pimp. That fool is as close as she come to having anybody."

"What's his name?" I said.

"Sylvester," Baby Richard said. "But he gonna make you call him Sly." Then he laughed again, long and hard. He was slapping his thighs and wiping away tears as I walked back to my car.

Twenty-two

"CAN you give me a ride?" M&M said. She was standing near my car door, shifting from foot to foot.

"Sure," I said. "Where do you need to go?"

"I have to go check up on my daughter," she said. "The woman who usually watches her at night is sick so I had to leave her home."

"How old is she?" I said, opening the car door for her.

"Four." She slipped into the passenger seat and slammed the door.

"Four?" I said when I got into my own seat. "You left a four-year-old home alone?"

"My neighbor listens for her," she said defensively. "The walls are paper thin, she can hear Tiffany cough in her sleep. Nothing is going to happen to her. Anyway, I only ever leave her when I can't drop her at the babysitter's house."

I shook my head. The last thing M&M was going to listen to was a lecture on proper parenting. And what was I going to do? Report her to the department of social services? Then what? The girl would be taken away from her mother and put into foster care, where her chances of suffering outright abuse were significantly higher. What was worse, occasional neglect or an increased chance of abuse? I wished I knew the answer to that.

As I drove down Figueroa, following M&M's directions, I said, "Do you know Sly, Violetta's pimp?"

"That creep. Yeah, I know him."

"You don't like him?"

"Nobody likes Sylvester," she said. "He's a pig."

"What was Violetta's relationship with him? Had she worked for him for a while?"

M&M shook her head. "Violetta used to work for a real sweet guy named Johnnie Brown. Johnnie was killed about a year ago."

"How?"

"He was shot in a robbery. He got jumped by a couple of guys, and he pulled his gun out. They got it off of him and shot him, just like that. Right in front of everybody. How do you like that? Shot by his own gun."

"Did the police ever find out who did it?"

She laughed. "We all knew who did it. They were just a couple of kids, you know? Looking for some money."

"Were they arrested?"

She shrugged. "I don't know. I don't think so. I mean, not for killing Johnnie. I think they got busted for something else."

"What were their names?"

She compressed her lips, shrugged, and stared out the window.

"Mary Margaret," I said. "They might have had something to do with Violetta's death."

"They couldn't have," she said. "By the time Violetta was killed they were both gone."

"Won't you tell me their names, just to be sure?"

She shook her head. "I don't know their names. I just saw them around, you know? I didn't know them or nothing."

I sighed and changed my line of questioning. "So after Johnnie was killed, Violetta went with Sly?"

"It's right up there." She pointed to a ramshackle apartment building, four stories, with a broken fire escape dangling from the roof. "That's where I live."

I pulled to a stop in front of the building.

M&M opened the door and then turned to me, holding it halfway open. "After Johnnie was killed, Violetta had this idea that she wouldn't go with anyone, you know? That she'd be on her own, keep all her money herself. Well, they won't allow that. If one girl did that then we all might, and where would they be then? They all got together, all of them, Sly and Baby Richard and a bunch of others, and they beat the hell out of her. They beat her really bad. She lost a couple of teeth, her face was real smashed up, and her side hurt, right here." M&M pressed her ribcage. "I think they broke some ribs."

"Did she go to the hospital?"

She shook her head. "No. She just holed up in her room for a week or so. I brought her food, because otherwise she wouldn't have had the money to eat. I even brought her . . ." Here M&M's voice trailed off.

"What did you bring her?"

"Nothing really. Just a little flea powder. It's all I could get. But it worked for the pain, you know? She was aching all over."

Flea powder—weak heroin, cut with all sorts of nasty stuff. That couldn't have helped Violetta heal.

"After that, that was when she went with Sly. She knew she had to, or the next time they'd kill her. It's not worth it. It's good with a pimp. You get to keep some of your money, enough to live on. And the others leave you alone. Some of them can be real good to you. Baby Richard, he takes good care of his girls."

I frowned skeptically. I could not help glancing at the still-red bite mark on her bosom. Her hand fluttered up to cover it and she laughed nervously.

"This was just silly, you know. He was mad at me. And the truth is, I could have got the guy to go for more. I was just being lazy and spending too much time worrying about Tiffany instead of my work. Baby Richard's a good man, you know? He buys Tiffany presents all the time. Last week he bought her brand new sneakers. And not Payless. Adidas."

I left that alone. Whatever she needed to believe to get through her day. I turned the subject back to Violetta. "Could Sly have had anything to do with her murder?" I asked.

M&M shrugged. "I don't know. I don't remember seeing him that night. He's got a usual parking spot, and I don't think his car was there, but I could be wrong. I wasn't looking for him, you know?"

"Baby Richard says he drives a white Chevy."

She twisted her mouth in disgust. "A real beater. All scratched up. I sat in it once, and there's a hole in the floor, you can see right into the road. Baby Richard used to have a Mercedes, and he's going to get a Navigator."

I wondered if the prostitutes on the street compared their pimps' rides the way some of the children in Ruby's school compared their parents', turning up their noses at vehicles like my stinky minivan and casting appreciative eyes on the German-made luxury sedans.

"I better go in," M&M said. "I don't have much time and I want to make sure Tiffy's okay. She had a runny nose when I put her to bed, and I'm a little worried she might have started running a fever."

She got out of the car, and slammed the door behind her. I pushed the button and rolled down the window.

"M&M," I called.

She had her key out and was fighting with the lock on the building's front door.

"You've got my number," I said. "You can always call me if you need anything, okay?"

Her lips turned up, revealing a set of small teeth. I realized that I had never before seen her smile. Her whole face softened and she suddenly looked years younger. Like a girl. She waved and the door opened, shutting with a thud behind her.

Twenty-three

IT was too late to go back and look for Sly. And frankly, I just didn't have it in me to talk to anyone else that night, especially the man who had beaten Violetta into turning over her money to him.

When I got home I was suddenly so grateful for Peter's odd hours, for the comfort of finding him awake and working when I walked through the door at one A.M.

While I was in the shower standing under a burning hot stream, trying to cleanse myself of the imaginary grime of Baby Richard and his revolting laughter, Peter made me a cup of chamomile tea.

"I was worried about you," he said as he tucked me into bed.

"You're sweet, Peter," I said, sipping my tea. "You're sweet, and kind. I'm so grateful to you." And then I burst into tears.

Peter got in bed next to me, pulling me close. He didn't say anything, just held me in his arms while I cried. I pressed my face against his soft T-shirt. Finally, when I was too tired to cry anymore, I sat up.

"Thanks," I said.

"My pleasure," he replied, and kissed me softly on the lips.

He didn't go back to work. I needed him, and it turned out he needed me. Or wanted me, or both.

Afterward we laid side-by-side, sweat cooling on our bodies.

"Are you going to be okay?" Peter said. "On this case, I mean?"

I nodded. "Yeah, I think so. It's no worse than any other, I guess. It's just, you know. My life is so much better than those women's. I feel . . . I don't know."

"The guilt of the privileged class?"

I smiled. "I guess you could put it like that."

"Life sure as hell isn't fair, is it?" Peter said.

"Nope. Life is definitely not fair."

IN the morning, I made the kids French toast. I even cooked a special piece for Sadie, made with egg yolks and some defrosted breast milk, much to Ruby's and Isaac's horror.

"She's not supposed to have egg whites or milk yet," I explained.

"That is so gross, Mama," Ruby said.

"Gross," Isaac affirmed. "Can I taste it?"

I ruffled his hair. "No, you can't taste it, you nut." I minced Sadie's French toast into little pieces, cut up some banana to go along with it, and placed her plate in front of her. I drowned the other kids' pieces in maple syrup and watched them gorge themselves.

"I love you guys," I said.

"I love you, too, Mama," Isaac replied.

Ruby said something unintelligible, her mouth full. Then she swallowed and said, "Is today a holiday?"

"No, I don't think so." I looked at the calendar taped to the fridge. "Nope, no holiday. Just a regular Saturday. Why?"

"Because you're being so nice to us."

"Eat your food, Ruby," I said.

Peter shuffled into the kitchen, his hair on end. He gave me a languid and satisfied smile and said, "Yummy, French toast."

Before I could stop him, he picked up a piece from Sadie's plate and popped it in his mouth. "Delicious," he announced.

Ruby turned bright red, laughing so hard she nearly choked on her mouthful of food. Isaac yelped, but I silenced him with a wink.

I smiled at Peter. "Let me give you your own, sweetie," I said and hurriedly dumped the remaining slices on a plate and placed it on the table in front of him. "Have some syrup."

By now Ruby and Isaac were nearly hysterical, kicking each other under the table and laughing so hard that tears rolled down their faces.

"What's with them?" Peter said.

"They're just being silly," I said as I poured him some coffee. "They're just a couple of silly geese."

Twenty-four

BY now I knew the way to the corner on Figueroa so well I'd even figured out a shortcut, longer in actual mileage, but one that cut down on traffic lights and busy main roads. I left my house at 8:30 at night and was pulling my car into a space by 9:00. Violetta's pimp was right where they said he'd be, sitting in the front seat of his old white Chevy Impala, pulled up right at the corner, where he could keep an eye on the women as they stood in the street, their hips cocked to one side, their pelvises pushed forward, their eyes on the cars that crawled slowly past.

I walked over to the car, took a breath, and bent down to look in the open passenger-side window. I was conscious at that moment of looking like the hookers did when they leaned into the cars and offered themselves, and I felt a flush creep across my cheeks.

"Sylvester?" I said.

"My name is Sly!" he snarled, but there was something almost perfunctory about his anger, as if he'd been correcting people about his name for a good long time.

"Sorry," I said. "Sly. I'm a private investigator working for Violetta Spees's family, and I was hoping you might give me a few minutes of your time."

"Who you working for?"

"Violetta Spees's sister."

"I don't know no Violetta Spees." He stared straight ahead, looking up the street through the windshield, ignoring me.

"Really? How curious. My understanding is that she worked for you."

He shook his head. "Nope. Don't know nobody by that name."

"Look, I'm not a cop; I can't arrest you. I'm just trying to find out a little more about Violetta's last days, so that her mother can rest easy about what her daughter was doing. The poor woman is distraught now, worrying that Violetta might have been sick or in pain. So if you could just tell me a little about what you know, it would go a long way toward reassuring them."

This had to be the lamest thing I'd ever come up with. But getting Sly to admit that Violetta worked for him might be enough to convince Detective Jarin to take a look at him. Maybe even pull him in for questioning, get a warrant for a DNA sample. Not that I had high hopes for the latter. If Sly was responsible for Violetta's death, it would likely have had nothing to do with sex. She might have worked the whole night, turning tricks, before Sly gave her the last beating of her short life.

"Come on in here," Sly said. He leaned over and opened the door. When he turned to me I could see that his left eye was larger than his right. It was unfocused, not fixed on me as the other one was, but rolled ever so slightly to the side. I backed away from the door. "Come on," he said. "I don't want to shout. Just come on inside where we can talk."

The driver's seat was pushed way back, to accommodate his long legs. He'd reclined it as far as it could go, so that despite the length of his arms, he had to lean far forward to reach the door. He was light skinned, the honey-yellow color of cheap maple wood. His hair was cut close to his scalp and his eyes narrowed as he stared at me. He plastered a false smile on his face. "Come on in and we can talk."

"I can hear you just fine," I said. "How long had Violetta been working for you before she died?"

Suddenly, before I realized what was happening, he sprang across the seat and grabbed my arm. His hands were so big that they wrapped easily around my whole arm. He jerked me toward the open door and I stumbled, falling half in and half out of the car. I batted at him with my hands, trying to pull his fingers off my arm. He grabbed the back of my neck with his other hand and pulled me farther into the car. By now I was screaming, kicking against the doorway, trying to get purchase with my feet so I could pull myself out of the car. I jammed one knee against the doorframe and yanked my head back. His fingers dug into my neck from the back, reaching around almost to the front. I knew if he got his hand entirely around my throat he could kill me.

"What you doing to this girl?" a woman's voice shouted from the other side of the car. "Don't you know Baby Richard likes this girl? He gave her permission to be out here asking questions. What the hell you doing, fool? Baby Richard going to kill you if you hurt this girl."

The fingers around my neck loosened for a moment, and I reared back, jerking myself free and out of the car. He still held my arm in his viselike grip. On the other side of the car, her face framed by the driver's side window, was the woman in the purple dress, the woman who had hugged me and thanked me for saving them all from the murderer who had been killing them for so long.

"Let her go, Sylvester, or I'm a tell Baby Richard what you doin'."

He dropped my arm and I leapt back onto the curb.

The woman lifted her head out of the window and looked across the roof of the car. "You come with me," she said firmly. She started walking briskly, moving faster than I ever could have on such high heels. "Just keep walking," she whispered when I caught up to her. "Don't run. Where's your car at?"

I pointed to the side street where I'd parked my minivan. I didn't trust my voice.

"Get your keys ready."

I took them out of my jacket pocket and we broke into a run. I heard tires screech behind us as we turned the corner. We bolted as fast as we could, and for the first time I realized what automatic door locks were made for. I pointed the control at the car, and we flung ourselves inside just as Sly was turning the corner. I slammed the car into drive and pounded the accelerator to the floor, pulling out of the parking space with a scream of metal as I scratched my bumper along the car in front of us. Who would have thought a minivan could handle so well? I spun us around a corner, never lifting my foot off the gas for even a moment, and tore away down Figueroa.

"Is he still behind us?" I asked, breathlessly.

My savior turned and looked through the rear window. "I don't think so."

I kept driving, glancing back into the rearview mirror. When I was finally reassured that he wasn't there, I eased up a little. "Thank you. Thank you so much. I honestly thought he was going to kill me."

She shook her head. "I'm a have some explaining to do when Baby Richard hears I been throwing his name around like that."

"Are you going to be okay? Is he going to hurt you?"

She shook her head again. "He'd never hurt me. He knows I'd tell his mother, and then he be in worse trouble than he can stand."

"His *mother*?"

"My sister, Patrice. I'm Baby Richard's auntie. Auntie Jacqueline. Although out on the street, he don't call me that. When I'm working, he calls me Jackie, like everyone else."

"He's your nephew?" I said. "Your nephew is your pimp?"

She sighed. "Don't let's talk about that, now, okay? You hungry? Let's stop at that IHOP up there and get us some pancakes."

Twenty-five

BLUEBERRY pancakes and bacon sitting in a pool of syrup and melted butter are the perfect comfort food. I hadn't planned on ordering anything, but Jackie wouldn't let me sit and watch her eat. It made her self-conscious, she said. Purely to keep her company I told the waitress to bring me what she was having, but when the plate was set before me I dug in with enthusiasm.

With my mouth full, I said, "I don't know how to thank you, Jackie. You saved my life."

She waved her hand dismissively. "Oh, he wouldn't a killed you. He would a roughed you up a little, but he wouldn't kill a white woman in front of a block full of witnesses. Not even Sylvester's that much of a fool."

I rubbed the back of my neck. "Well, whatever he

would have done wouldn't have felt good, that much I know." I tenderly felt at what I knew would soon be purpling bruises. "He just moved himself up to suspect number one in Violetta's murder."

Jackie took a huge bite of pancake and folded half a strip of bacon into her mouth. Once she was done chewing she said, "I don't know about Violetta, but I do know he killed a woman once. I know that for sure."

I put down my fork. "Sylvester killed someone?"

"One a his hos. She went behind his back with some other guy, I don't know who. She was even giving her money to this other man. Sly heard about it, and he pulled her right off the street. He beat her up and then he kicked her so hard and so many times that she died. Right there, right in the alley behind the Dunkin' Donuts."

The pancakes lay in a clotted indigestible mass in the pit of my stomach. "He kicked her to death?" I said, my voice thick with nausea.

"Kicked her right to death. He evil, that Sylvester. And he a coward, too. Would never a fight a man, but he happy to kill a woman."

"What was her name?"

Jackie shook her head. "It was before I turned out, so I didn't know her. I heard about it from someone who saw it, though."

"Who told you?"

She frowned, trying to remember. "I don't know. Teeny, maybe?"

"Teeny who was killed by Charles Towne?"

"Yeah." She took a last bite of pancake, scraped her fork through a puddle of syrup, and licked the tines with her small pink tongue, like a cat.

"When did this happen?" I said.

She shrugged. "Well, I been out almost ten years now. So longer ago than that."

I sighed, my hopes for a conviction of Sly for this earlier murder evaporating. More than ten years ago was too long, especially if the only witness was a dead woman. I would have to talk Detective Jarin into bringing Sly in for Violetta's murder. I hoped the assault on me would carry some weight in convincing the detective that Sly warranted a closer look.

"Do you know Sylvester's last name?" I said.

"Do snakes have last names? I always figured he just sprung up out the earth. Everybody just calls him Sylvester, or Sly, if he can make them say it."

After we ate, Jackie had me drive her back to the taco truck, where Baby Richard would provide her with the protection that she paid for. She assured me that she was in no danger, that Sly would never hurt another man's woman, especially not her. I let her out at the curb, and watched her stroll over to her nephew. Together they glanced back at me and waved. How I had ended up protected by Baby Richard, I could only begin to guess. I think what it came down to was that Jackie's saying so made it true.

First thing Monday morning, after a fitful couple of nights, I called Robyn and told her about Sylvester.

"I think he murdered Violetta," I said. "But it's just a

feeling, and I'm worried about trying to convince Detective Jarin to bring him in based on a feeling."

"It's more than a feeling," Robyn said. "The creep attacked you."

"Yeah, and that's good, but it's not enough."

"That's *good?*"

"You know what I mean." I related the story about the hooker Jackie told me about. "It could be just a rumor," I said. "Maybe there never was a beating behind the Dunkin' Donuts, or maybe there was but the woman didn't die. I don't know. But if you could do a search of unsolved cases looking for a prostitute beaten to death sometime before 1995, I could just skip Jarin altogether and go directly to Detective Sherman in the cold case unit."

"Okay," she said. "I'll see what I can do, and I'll try to do it fast. Where will you be today, if I can find the information?"

"I just dropped the kids off at school, but I'm heading home now. You can call me there."

What she did, of course, was call her father. Al didn't bother to call me. About an hour after I hung up the phone with his daughter, he showed up at my house.

"What're you doing here?" I said, when I opened the door.

"What am I doing here? That's how you greet me?" He pushed by me and into the house. I followed him down the hall, through the ballroom and into the kitchen.

"You got coffee?" he said.

"I was just making a pot for Peter. He should be up pretty soon. He takes it pretty strong."

Al shrugged. I poured him a cup and watched him ladle spoonfuls of sugar into it. His motions were jerky, like he was restraining himself. I'd seen him angry, but never like this.

"What's up, Al? Is something wrong?"

"Is something wrong?" he repeated.

"Yeah, is something wrong? You seem, I don't know, wound up."

He smacked his dirty teaspoon down on the table, sending up a spray of coffee. "You're damn right there's something wrong!" he shouted. He was still yelling when Peter stumbled into the kitchen.

"What the hell is going on here?" Peter said. "Is it too much to ask to be able to get some sleep in this house?"

Al, who had paused in mid-holler when Peter staggered in, said, "It's 10:30 in the morning."

"You know he works at night, Al," I said, trying to keep my voice calm and level, as I had since he began his tirade.

"Coffee," said Peter. "Good." He poured himself a cup and took a deep gulp. "Now, like I said, what the hell is going on here?"

Al turned to Peter. "Do you have any idea where your wife is spending her nights? Do you know what she's been up to?"

Peter nodded. "I know she's spending them driving around godforsaken South Central. Why? I thought you went with her."

"I went with her *once*. I did not go with her the other night when she nearly got herself killed by a murdering pimp."

"Juliet?" Peter said. "What is he talking about?"

It took all morning to calm them down. It's hard to say who was angrier, my husband or my partner. For the first time since I'd introduced them eight years before, they were in complete agreement about something, and that something was what a fool I was, what unnecessary risks I took, and how furious they were with me. Every time I thought I'd put the fire out, reassured them that I would never again go to Figueroa Street, that I'd never drive *by* that part of Figueroa Street, one of them would start up again and set the whole cycle of recrimination and abject apology going one more time.

Robyn, whose fault it was that I was in this position to begin with, finally released me from it. She called just as Peter was describing, in the detail only a writer of horror films could, exactly what Sylvester would have done to me if I hadn't been lucky enough to be rescued by Jackie.

"Hey, Robyn," I said. "Thanks for getting your dad on my case."

"Somebody needs to be on your case, Juliet. You think you're a cop, but you don't have the most important tool in a cop's arsenal."

"What's that? A .357 Magnum?"

"No, backup."

That one word, more than all of Al and Peter's shouting and cursing, took me aback. Because it was true, I went down there all on my own, without backup. Worst of all, once I was there, when things got dicey, I forced someone to act as my backup, and I had no idea what the ramifications of that act would be for her. Jackie had spoken so carelessly about her immunity from Sylvester's violence, but I had no idea if that was true. For all I knew, for all *she* knew, she could be in terrible danger. And I had put her there.

I had to get that man off the street.

"What did you find?" I said.

"I found two possibles. A Sheila Jones who was killed in 1991, cause of death was internal injuries from a beating. And a Jane Doe, 1990, also beaten. Both those cases are unsolved."

A sudden horrible thought crossed my mind. "Do you think this could be another serial killer? That either Sylvester or someone else killed them and then killed Violetta?"

"These two cases look really different from one another. The Jane Doe was a horrifically violent sexual assault, and the Jones case looks like a robbery. Her purse and jewelry were gone. Someone tore a gold necklace off her neck, breaking the clasp and leaving a few links. I suppose that could have happened after she died; bodies get robbed sometimes, but the fact that there's no sexual assault in this case makes me think they're different killers."

Neither of them sounded much like Violetta's murder, either. I jotted down the details anyway. When I hung up I found Peter and Al commiserating over the Dodgers draft picks. Clearly their shared rage had been a bonding experience for them. I'd never seen them quite so friendly before. Usually the most they could muster for one another was polite disinterest.

I called Detective Sherman, finding him at his desk. His reaction to my antics of the night before was not much more positive than my husband's and Al's had been. He modulated his volume, but the hectoring tone was the same.

"Jesus!" I said finally. "Okay, I get it. I was an idiot for going down there, and I'll never do it again. Now will you please let me tell you about Sylvester?"

"Hm," he said when I was done.

"Yeah, I know. It's not much. But if you have some physical evidence from those two cases, maybe you can check it out."

"This isn't enough to bring him in, Juliet," the detective said. "Not for the old cases. I can't make an arrest based on unsubstantiated rumor. No judge will issue the warrant."

"I figured as much," I said.

"I like him better for your client's murder," he said. "He's her pimp, he's got a reputation for violence. It's enough to justify a conversation. You know what, I'll give that detective a call. What was his name? Gordon?"

"Jarin."

"Yeah, Jarin. I remember him from before I moved out of the 77th Division. I could never remember his name back then, either."

Relieved I wouldn't have to speak to the man myself, I said, "You can tell him to call me if he wants."

"I'll do that. Now, will you promise me one thing? Will you promise me that you'll just leave it alone now, let us do our jobs?"

"I promise I won't go questioning dangerous men on Figueroa Street anymore, how about that?"

"Good enough," the detective said.

Twenty-six

PETER and I picked the kids up from school together that afternoon, much to their delight. I didn't tell them that the only reason Daddy was along for the ride was because he no longer trusted Mama not to put their lives and her own on the line. I punished him, though. He had forgotten, if he'd ever known, that Monday was Tae Kwon Do.

"Do you just sit here?" he said, after we'd wrapped the kids in their belts and sent them into their classes. Ruby was a green belt, and Isaac was struggling to work his way out of Mighty Mites.

"Yup."

"You can't go for coffee or something?"

"Nope. There's nothing close."

"How is that possible? This must the only corner in the city of Los Angeles without a Starbucks on it."

"Don't worry, honey," I said sweetly. "We'll pass the time by chatting with the other mommies."

Peter groaned. Two women joined us on the bench. I knew them by sight, but not by name. A third, Karyan, whose son Jirair was in Isaac's class, came over, too. She greeted me warmly, and I introduced her to Peter.

"You're the screenwriter," she said.

"Yes," he said.

"We don't believe in cinema."

"Excuse me?" he asked.

I suppressed my smile.

Karyan continued, "My husband and I don't believe in cinema. We think it's a destructive force. In fact, we think that most of society's ills can be blamed directly on the mass media. No offense."

"None taken," he said.

"So what's new, Karyan?" I asked. "How are you doing? Did you find a nanny yet?"

"I thought I had," she said. "We hired a Brazilian woman; she seemed fine in the interview, and came with wonderful references." She shuddered. "It just shows how meaningless those are."

"What happened?" one of other women asked.

"I caught her on her first day alone with the children doing the most awful things."

"What?" the woman whispered, breathless. Her fascination was downright prurient. Like she was listening to nanny porn.

"First, she used our CD player, which my husband expressly told her not to touch. It's a very fine and sophisticated system, and not meant to be played with."

"That *is* appalling," Peter said. I stomped delicately on his toe.

"She put on this Brazilian music, I don't know, *samba* or something." Karyan shuddered again. "The whole time she was cleaning the house this music was blaring. I can't even imagine what the neighbors thought. Then, when the baby got up, she microwaved his bottle! When I hired her I told her a half dozen times, never microwave the bottles. If you don't have time to use the stove, you can microwave the milk in a glass measuring cup, stir it thoroughly, and pour it into the bottle."

"Why can't you microwave the bottles?" Peter said.

I said, "Because plastic leaches dioxins that cause cancer."

Karyan nodded. "And also the microwave heats unevenly and tiny bubbles of boiling milk can sear through the top of the baby's mouth and into her brain."

"What?" Peter asked. "That's ridiculous. That's the most—"

This time I stomped less delicately.

Karyan ignored him. "The final straw was when she put her cup of coffee right on the table next to the baby. He could have pulled it over and scalded himself. He could have ended up in the burn unit! That did it for me. I can't have someone like that working for me."

"How do you know all this?" Peter asked. "Were you peeking from behind a door or something?"

"Of course I wasn't peeking, what do you think I am?" Karyan said. "I saw it all on the nannycam."

"The nannycam?"

One of the other mothers explained to Peter, "It's a little motion-activated camera hidden in the house. We've got two, one in my daughter's bedroom and the other in the kitchen. It's really ingenious; they can hide them anywhere. We have one in a stuffed bear and another that looks like a cookie jar."

"You people have hidden cameras spying on your children's babysitters?" Peter said.

Karyan took umbrage at the horror in his voice. "Of course we do. Anyone who loves their children would. How else are you going to know what's going on when you're not there?"

Peter sighed and then looked at me. "When does the class end?" he asked.

"Not for a little while. Why don't you take a walk?" I suggested.

When he was gone I turned to Karyan and shrugged. "What can I say?"

She waved a dismissive hand. "Don't worry, Juliet. He's a husband. That's all you need to say."

As we drove home, the kids safely buckled into their booster seats, Sadie whimpering with frustration at having to face the rear of the car in her car seat, Peter said, "You don't seriously think it's okay to spy on your nanny, do you?"

"Of course not," I said. "I think it's nuts, and depressing, but I can totally understand the impulse."

I explained to Peter my theory of the panic of contemporary child-rearing. In a society saturated by media, we know in exquisite detail all the risks of childhood. We know about the dangers that lurk outside our doors, and those that lurk inside our houses. We are aware of what sometimes happens when an infant swallows an almond or a bite of hot dog. We understand the risk of iron poisoning from eating a parent's vitamin pill. We have heard of children who have been the victims of improperly installed car seats. We are warned about the risks to our precious children of eating strawberries before age one and of bicycle-riding without a helmet. There are a variety of forces at play in this culture of peril. Our constant access to news of all kinds, television stations that must find something to fill a twenty-four-hour news broadcast and some way to lure viewers. The litigiousness of our society, which demands that all harms be rectified by the assignment of blame and the awarding of cash. All this is exacerbated by the fact that the infant mortality rate for certain children is so low. Where once childhood was considered a perilous journey with no sure guarantee of arrival on the shores of adulthood, now we expect and demand that every child make the voyage safely, even those born so young and so small that they fit in the palm of our hands. Every child, that is, except those born in poverty to people of color.

Add to these factors educated and competent mothers trained for professions they no longer practice, who have turned aside from the futures they once expected for themselves to focus their attention and ambition solely on their children. These children are valuable beyond measure, because we've sacrificed ourselves for them and to them. We now understand that we are as able and skilled as men, that we can do the work of the market-place as well as they can, but we have left that work to raise these children, not because we have to—most of us—but because we want to. These children must be worth our sacrifice, they must be extraordinary, and they must be safe. We cannot risk the possibility of anything happening to the precious focus of our lives.

For those mothers who have not willingly paid the professional price, guilt provides the same motivating force. It ratchets up the value of their children so that harm to them is intolerable, and all too easily imagined.

"So what are you saying?" Peter said as we led the children up the stone steps to our house, his hand resting on the new banister we had installed because the old one had bars just far enough apart to fit a child's head in between. "Are you saying that our parents and grandparents didn't value and love their children as much as we value and love ours?"

"No. I'm saying that their love was less complicated by guilt and fear, and by a sense of the price paid for it."

"I don't know, Juliet. I think your parents are pretty adept at the guilt thing."

"They are adept at making *me* feel guilty. I don't think they necessarily feel much of it themselves. Or if they do, it's about larger things."

"I'm not convinced it's limited to our generation. When I was in elementary school I knew a kid, Paul

Scofield, whose mother was a complete headcase. She used to dress him in sweaters in the middle of the summer because she was afraid he'd get a cold. She used to make him wear a football helmet when he rode his bicycle or even when we played baseball in the park. She walked him to school and picked him up. Every day for lunch he would get these crazy sandwiches all on homemade bread with, like, tofu on them. He always tossed his lunch and begged off the rest of us. After a while my mom started packing me two Fluffernutters just so Paul wouldn't starve."

"You've proved my point," I said. "His mother was a headcase, right? She was a nut, totally different from the norm. Well, how many of Ruby's friends eat only organic food? Their lunch is all natural almond butter on organic bread, spread with jelly made from organic grapes with no sugar added. That's if they're even allowed to have nuts at all, because of the danger of developing an allergy. They wear their helmets when they ride their bikes, their backpacks don't have their names printed on the outside so that a predator won't be able to trick them by pretending to know them. Not that this is an issue, because they never *ever* walk to or from school alone."

Peter frowned thoughtfully. "So what you're saying is that what was once considered crazy is now just normal."

"Exactly. If you *don't* do those things you're crazy. A cautious and decent parent would never let her child do sports without pads and helmets or walk to school alone. You wouldn't, would you?"

We were standing in the ballroom and we both looked

over at the pile of bicycles, scooters, and skateboards in the corner. Arrayed next to them were helmets, wrist guards and kneepads.

"You see," I said. "We've all turned into poor Paul Scofield's mother. What happened to him, by the way?"

"Paul? He was a huge pot dealer in college. Another guy from our class went to Humboldt State up in northern California. He used to send Paul a package every month. Paul's mother never asked where he got the money for his car; she just made him buy a Volvo."

I looked over at Ruby, who was snapping on her helmet as she straddled her pink and purple bicycle. "Jeez," I said.

Peter said, "I don't think he kept it up in medical school, though."

"Medical school?"

"Yeah, last I heard he was doing a psychiatry residency in New York City."

"It's nice he could keep the same job, more or less."

"What do you mean?"

"Drug distribution," I said. "Helping people alter their consciousness. Back then it was pot, now it's Prozac."

Twenty-seven

Two days later I heard from Detective Sherman.

"Sylvester Waters," he said. "That's your man, I think. Unless there are two pimps operating out of the Figueroa Street corridor named Sylvester."

"Do you have a physical description?" I asked. I was at work in Al's garage, trying to put together my hours for the month so Chiki could prepare the bills.

"Black, forty-one years old, six foot four. A glass left eye."

"That's him," I said.

"I'll look at him for those old cases you sent me. But I have bad news for you on Violetta Spees."

"What?"

"Sylvester Waters was in county serving a thirty-day drug possession sentence on the day she was killed."

I put my head in my hands. I had been so sure he was the one. "Are you sure? Could there be any mistake?"

"Don't think so," Detective Sherman said. "I mean, I've heard of guys arrested in a case of mistaken identity, and even made to do someone else's time, but it's not real common."

I must have groaned out loud because the detective said, "If you want I can arrest him on an assault and battery charge. You've got a witness, right?"

"I don't want to put her in the position of having to give a statement. And even if he gets convicted, a judge isn't going to sentence him to any time for grabbing me."

"You never know."

"No," I said. "But you'll look at him for those old murders?"

The detective said, "Yeah, I'll dig around a little. It's going to come down to finding a witness. I've got to at least find someone who can connect him with one or the other of the victims. Someone who can verify if he was pimping for them."

"That's not going to be easy."

"Nope. Especially since the murders were so long ago. Finding someone around who remembers these women is going to be hard. It's not a lifestyle known for its longevity. But cold cases are all I do. It's hardly a unique problem for this unit to be dealing with."

I thanked the detective. In all my dealings with the LAPD I had never come across a cop so helpful, so friendly, and so untroubled by the fact that I was a private investigator. As a rule the police do not like the members of our profession. They resent our intrusion. This is true even in the cases where a sheriff's department will contract out an investigation to a private firm, which happens not infrequently. But Detective Sherman seemed to suffer from none of these biases. Perhaps he recognized in me something of a kindred spirit. We both had a little bit of the pit bull in us. Like me, he was unable to give up on a case or a problem until he'd seen it through to the bitter end.

Al and Chiki looked at me expectantly. They were almost as frustrated as I was when I told them we were back at square one. I think Al had been looking forward to me wrapping this up and moving on to something a little more lucrative.

I turned back to my white board and crossed Sylvester's name off. I'd already drawn a thick line through Baby Richard.

"Now what?" Chiki said.

I turned to my columns. Tricks, Boyfriends, Coworkers, Family. I was right back where I started. The Tricks category was where I was most likely to find Violetta's murderer, and the one category I had no real way of really exploring. I looked down the other lists. My eye settled on a name. Ronnie.

"Now I go to San Diego," I said.

Twenty-eight

IT took us six hours to drive to San Diego from Los Angeles, about three times what it would have taken me on my own. On my own, I would not have had to stop three times for bathroom breaks, another for a clothes change, another to buy a new audio book, another for a mid-morning meal, and half a dozen times for vomiting false alarms. On my own, I would not have insisted on staying in a hotel equidistant from Legoland and the San Diego Zoo.

It was while I was on my knees in the back of the minivan, trying to breathe through my nose as I sprayed Febreze over the vomit spattered seats, that I really regretted my idea that we turn my trip to interview Ronnie into a brief family vacation.

"The lines will be shorter if we go midweek," I had said to Peter. "We haven't gone on a family vacation in ages, since before Sadie was born. In a few years we won't be able to pull them out of school without worrying that they'll miss something important."

So there we were, waiting in line for half an hour to get strapped onto something that looked like an elaborate, brightly colored sawhorse. Everything in Legoland was brightly colored; it was a cacophony of primary colors, true blues and screaming reds, yellows brighter than the sun and greens so verdant they made AstroTurf look pale by comparison.

"Do you really think this is a good idea, Isaac?" I said. "You couldn't keep your French fries down in the car, why do you think you'll be able to keep from throwing up on a roller coaster?"

"It's not a roller coaster," he said.

"Yes it is."

"It's connected at the top, not the bottom."

"It's just a different kind of roller coaster."

Peter said, "He'll be fine, it's barely a ride. It's nowhere near as scary as Thunder Mountain, right, Isaac?"

"It's not the scary part I'm worrying about," I said.

By then we were at the front of the line and the kids and Peter were being strapped in. I moved aside to let the couple behind us go, but I think they'd been listening to our conversation.

"No thanks," the young man said. "We'll wait for the next one."

Another father too far behind us to hear our nausea-related conversation pushed forward. I moved out of the line to the exit rail, pushing Sadie along in her stroller. She stared up at the web of rails, enraptured. I suddenly remembered something I'd read about a man getting hit on the head and killed by a shoe dropped from a roller coaster, or maybe it was a leg sticking out. Something like that. I moved Sadie to a safe distance from the ride.

"Look, sweetie," I said. "Lego horsies."

Isaac looked only a little green when he disembarked, and Ruby was positively beaming.

We spent the next few hours in a mad rush of Lego, hopping from Lego boats to Lego cars to Lego animals, taking the kids' pictures next to Lego people, eating crappy fast food out of Lego-shaped boxes.

Finally, when they had ridden on every ride and scrambled across every bridge, I tapped Peter on the shoulder. "Honey," I said. "If I don't see an earth tone in about two minutes, my head is going to explode."

Over their vigorous protests, we hustled the team into the car, but not before caving in and buying a pile of the same Lego sets we could have bought at one of the dozens of toy stores within a few miles of our house. We made our way through rush hour traffic to our hotel, and within a couple of hours I had Sadie asleep in her portacrib, and Ruby and Isaac bathed, in their pajamas, and tucked side by side into a double bed watching a movie on SpectraVision that they'd only seen half a dozen times before. Peter was on the floor with the Lego sets, trying to build a space station without looking at the directions.

"Wouldn't it be easier if you followed the little book?" I said.

"The whole point is to figure out how to do it. If they *tell* you then it isn't any fun. They didn't have instruction manuals and Lego *sets* when I was a kid. They gave you a box of blocks and you did it yourself."

I made my voice sound like that of a crotchety old man. "Back in my day," I quivered, "we used to whittle our Lego pieces out of wood all by ourselves."

"Very funny. Don't you have somewhere to go?"

I leaned over and kissed him on the neck, digging my fingers in his side and tickling him.

"Stop it!" he shouted, laughing.

"Be quiet, Daddy!" Ruby said. "You're interrupting our movie."

"Yeah, you're interrupting their movie," I said, tickling him again. He batted my hand away.

I left them to their television and their toys and set off for Ronnie's dorm. He was not expecting me. I had not wanted to ask either Corentine or Heavenly for Ronnie's address, partly because I was worried that they would alert Ronnie to my visit, and partly because I knew they would be angry with me for pursuing this line of inquiry. I don't know how Chiki found the address (surely not on the computer) but he gave me a dorm name, a room number, and directions from the hotel.

What I didn't have was Ronnie. He wasn't in his room, his door was locked, and his hall was empty. I walked from room to room until I found a door through which I could hear the thumping beat of hip hop music.

I knocked, and when that had no result, pounded on the door. A young white man with blond floppy hair opened the door. He was shirtless, his baggy pants hanging off the bones of his pelvis and revealing three inches of plaid boxer shorts. His right shoulder was covered by a tattoo, a geometric face vaguely reminiscent of the Maori masks I remember seeing in a movie set in New Zealand.

"Yeah?" he said.

Over the blare of the music I asked if he knew where Ronnie Spees might be at this hour of the evening.

"Ronnie? He's at his girlfriend's. He, like, never sleeps here no more."

"Do you know where his girlfriend lives?" I said.

"Two floors down, at the end of the hall, last room before the bathrooms."

"What's her name?"

"Audrey, Audrey something."

I made my way downstairs. I'd entered the dorm behind two young women who unlocked the door and then, surely violating dorm rules, held it open for me. The door to Ronnie's girlfriend's hall was also locked, but another pleasant and careless young woman held the door for me.

"Which room is Audrey's?" I asked the girl who let me in.

She pointed me down the hall. There was music coming from this room also, so loud that the cheap plywood door trembled in the doorframe. I knocked and moments later Ronnie opened the door.

"Does nobody at UC San Diego wear a shirt?" I asked.

Ronnie had no tattoos, but there was a gold ring piercing his nipple. I must have stared at it because he fingered it gently, wincing.

"Me and Audrey got these the other day. Don't tell my mom, okay? She'll freak."

"I never would. Doesn't it hurt?"

He shrugged. "It's supposed to stop after a few days."

What, I wondered, would Ruby be piercing once she reached this age?

"Aren't you going to ask me in?"

He looked over his shoulder as if evaluating something in the room, then he held the door open for me.

Audrey looked about twelve years old. She was a wisp of a thing, skinny and short, with bitten nails painted an aggressive black. Her eyes were outlined in kohl, her eyebrow and nose were pierced with gold rings much thicker than the one through Ronnie's, and presumably her own, nipple. She was also blond, with skin so pale it seemed almost translucent. She was sitting on her bed, her knees bent and her scrawny arms wrapped around them.

"You must be Audrey," I said. "I'm Juliet. I'm a private detective." I turned to Ronnie. "Does she know about Violetta?"

He nodded. "Audrey and me got no secrets."

"I'm investigating Violetta's murder. Ronnie's sister Heavenly hired me."

Audrey nodded and glanced at her boyfriend. He scratched idly at the line of hair leading from his belly button into the top of his pants.

"Something going on at home?" Ronnie asked. He pulled over a desk chair and motioned for me to sit down. When I did, he stretched out on the bed next to Audrey, and she curled up against him.

"Not that I know of," I said. "My husband and I decided to take the kids on a vacation to San Diego. Legoland today and the zoo tomorrow. While I'm down here I thought I might take the opportunity to talk to you without your family around."

I glanced down at Audrey who was tracing one bitten nail in wide circles around Ronnie's nipple. He followed my gaze and grabbed her hand with his.

"Not now, baby," he said.

"Could we go somewhere to talk?" I asked.

He shrugged. "Like I said, Audrey and me got no secrets."

I wasn't so sure of that. "Well, what I was hoping to talk about was Violetta's last evening at your mother's house. When she . . ." I paused. "When you two argued. Are you sure you wouldn't rather do that in private?"

He looked up, sharply. Then he leaped gracefully up off the bed. "I'll be right back, baby. I got to talk to this lady for a little while."

Audrey's face collapsed in an expression of woe so exaggerated that for a moment I wondered if it was even real. Ronnie picked up a T-shirt off a pile on the floor and pulled it over his head. He leaned down and kissed her lingeringly on the lips. For a moment she wrapped her arms around his neck and lifted her body up toward him, but then he loosened them and she dropped back down on the bed. It was only when Ronnie and I were outside the dormitory and walking across the quad to a coffee shop that I realized I had not heard the girl utter a single word.

I paid for my cup of tea and for Ronnie's mocha with extra whipped cream. I was buying a lot of coffee for people on this case. I wished I had thought to keep track of my receipts. Jeanelle would have liked it if I could have billed Heavenly for expenses.

We took our drinks over to a small table some distance from where the other students were sitting chatting or hunched over schoolbooks and laptops.

"Heavenly and your mother told me that Violetta made a pass at you," I said. No point in beating around the bush.

He winced. "Nah. She didn't make a pass. She just . . . you know."

"I really don't."

"She just put her hands on me. You know," he motioned vaguely in the direction of his crotch. The light was dim, but I was fairly sure he was blushing.

"Why don't you tell me exactly what happened."

"Sounds like you know."

"I know what your mother and Heavenly said. I don't know what you saw or felt."

He rubbed his face with his hand and then took a sip of his drink, leaving a delicate white mustache of whipped cream. I fought the urge to wipe it off with my napkin.

"We were watching TV, and she started talking about how there was no room for her on the couch. Then she sat down on my lap. She started like, wiggling, you know? Like she was trying to get comfortable. She asked me do I like that, and then she reached down and just . . . you know . . . grabbed me. I jumped right up and yelled at her to stop it. She fell on the floor. First Mama got all crazy at me, hollering, 'Why you hurt your sister like that?' But when I said what Violetta had done, Mama tossed her out."

"Had she ever done anything like that before?"

He shrugged.

"She *had* done it before?"

"Not like that, no. That was the first time she, like, grabbed me right there. But she used to make jokes, you know? How big a man I was getting to be, whether I was getting any, that kind of thing."

"Did she do that kind of thing a lot?"

He shrugged again. "When she wasn't using or drinking, she'd be real sweet. She'd treat me no different than Chantelle does. Or even Heavenly. But Violetta could get real silly when she was high."

There was that word again. Silly.

"Was that the last time you saw her?"

He nodded.

"And the last time you talked to her?"

"No, she called me the next day. She was all crying, you know? Talking about how sad she was, and how sorry. She asked me to call Mama and tell her that she had apologized."

"And did you?"

He nodded. "Yeah, I called and just said, you know,

Violetta called me and she's real sorry about what happened yesterday. That's it."

"Do you know if your mother talked to her after that?"

He nodded. "Yeah, I think she did. She said she would, anyway."

"Your mother said she was planning on calling Violetta?"

"Yeah, my mother told me she was going to call Violetta and tell her that if she was really sorry, and if she promised to behave, she could come home, and Mama would try to help her get into rehab."

Poor Corentine, one more time opening up her heart and her home to her daughter, unable to close the door on the hope that Violetta would somehow manage to turn her life around. The eternal belief of a mother in the possibility of her child.

"Had you ever seen Violetta behave this way with anyone else?"

Ronnie laughed derisively. "My sister Violetta was a ho. She behaved that way with *everybody*. Even before she turned out, she'd be throwing herself at people. It didn't matter, as long as she thought she could get the drugs out of somebody, she'd push herself on him no matter who he was."

"That must have been embarrassing for you."

He gave a what-are-you-gonna-do flap of his hand. "It's no big thing. Some dudes, it's their mamas out there putting it out. Now, that would be bad."

"Still, it can't have been pleasant."

"Truth, I was happier when she went out on the street instead of just trying to do it in the neighborhood, you know? With my friends and such. It was almost better when she was out there for real."

"If she had come home, would you have been worried that she'd start up again, with your friends?"

"I don't know. Maybe. She'd have had to be straight if she wanted to come home, but then if she started looking for the stuff and got herself high, she'd probably just be the same old Violetta."

"Do you think she could have straightened herself out?"

He finished his drink and licked his lips. "I don't know," he said. "It's real hard, and I don't think I know anyone who's done it. Audrey's sister, she's been doing dope since she was fifteen, and she's been in rehab as often as she's been out of it. They're rich and they put her in those real expensive, private places, but it doesn't do any good. I don't see how Violetta could have done it all on her own if even a rich white girl can't."

He got to his feet and pushed his chair back. "I got to get back," he said. "Audrey gets nervous if I'm gone for too long."

I stood up, too.

"You know who I blame for that last night?" Ronnie said. "Thomas. He knew what Violetta was like when she was drinking. He didn't have any business bringing those beers over."

"But he didn't know she'd be there, did he? She surprised you all."

He frowned. "Even if that's true, he didn't have to let her have anything to drink. He didn't have to give her beer. He could have just said no."

"What was their relationship like? Hers and Thomas's?"

Ronnie clearly wanted to get away from the table and back to his clingy and silent girlfriend. "Nothing special. Same as her relationship with everyone, I guess."

"Same as with you?" I raised my eyebrows, meaningfully.

"You want to know that, you got to ask Thomas," Ronnie said.

Twenty-nine

OUR plan was to spend just a couple of hours at the zoo and get on the road back to Los Angeles in plenty of time to miss the traffic. That was the plan. I was tired of the dead ends this case was leading me to, and I wanted to hustle things along, get back to the city and pay a visit to Thomas, whom I'd never met, and if that led nowhere, finally concede defeat and refund Heavenly's retainer fee. That was the plan.

What was not part of the plan was panic. What was not part of the plan was standing with my back pressed against the polar bear tank, shrieking my daughter's name. What was not part of the plan was losing Ruby.

It started like this: Peter and I watched the polar bears glide by the huge windows, their yellowish fur brushing the glass, their massive paws paddling in an aquatic ballet. The window was underground, with a fish-eye view of the tank. We could watch the bears swim from underwater. It was hypnotic. Finally, when the people behind us began expressing their impatience too loudly to ignore, we gathered up Isaac, who had been kneeling at the window in front of us.

"Where's Ruby?" Peter said.

"She must be back at the first observation window." The viewing area was divided into bays, each fronting its own window. We walked back to the first bay looking for her small, red-headed figure. It took all of thirty seconds for us to shift from unconcern, to alarm, to out-and-out dread. We began running in and out of the exhibit, calling her name.

"Where is she?" I screamed at Peter.

He didn't bother to answer. The other families stared at us, their faces reflecting either concern or disapproval, depending on just how sanctimonious they were, or whether they'd ever been unlucky enough to find themselves in our shoes.

"A little red-haired girl," I said, frantically, to the crowd at large. "Has anyone seen a little red-haired girl? Seven years old?"

"What is she wearing?" a mother holding her toddler on a harness and leash asked me.

I stared at the leash for a moment and then replied, "I don't . . . I don't know."

"You don't know what your daughter is wearing?" she

said, horrified. Then she yanked on her child's leash and turned her back.

"Peter!" I yelled as I ran from the polar bear exhibit and out into the sun. "What was she wearing? What was Ruby wearing?"

Peter was standing on the path, his head whipping back and forth. He ran a few steps up each path and then, when he didn't see Ruby, tore back down. He carried Isaac in one arm and hauled the empty stroller behind him.

Sadie hung from my chest in the Baby Björn, my shoulders aching from the strain. Her legs danced against my belly as I ran after my husband.

"What was Ruby wearing?" I shouted again.

"Her yellow daisy T-shirt," he said. "Come on, let's go up the hill to the information booth. We'll find someone and ask them what to do."

We ran as fast as we could up the hill, our breath ragged in our chests, the stroller careening along in front of us, half of the time on two wheels. We bumped into people and didn't even bother to apologize, so fixated were we on making it to where we could ask for help.

These times are when I regret most my career in criminal defense. Knowing too much about the evil of which men are capable is a very bad thing when your child is missing. In the moments it took to climb to the zoo information booth I saw Ruby, my little girl, in the clutches of the worst kind of madman. The kind who lurks in places where children find themselves out from under their parents' eyes. The kind who snatches them up and steals them away. The kind who feeds off innocence and chews on the virtue of childhood. I saw all that, and more.

I saw myself, a woman who could not keep her child safe. Who could not protect her from the evil world. A woman who lost her child.

By the time we arrived at the information booth, I was crying too hard to speak.

Peter pushed aside a line of people waiting for maps and directions to the bathroom and grabbed the shirt-sleeve of the young woman manning the booth. "Our daughter. She's lost. Her name is Ruby. Please. Please help us."

"Ruby?" the young woman said.

"Yes, Ruby. She's seven years old."

She smiled broadly. "Little red-haired girl?"

"Yes! Yes!" I shouted through my tears.

"Oh, Ruby's doing fine. I bet she's having herself an ice cream cone about now."

"Ruby gets ice cream?" Isaac said. "That's not fair."

It seems that Ruby was never lost. She was just so prepared for the possibility of being lost, so well-schooled in the measures to take should she find herself lost that when she turned around in the polar bear exhibit and did not immediately see our faces, she began running up the paths, looking for someone in a uniform.

Before we'd even noticed her absence, Ruby had

stomped up the hill, announced herself as lost to the fresh-faced young woman (never ask a man, always look for a woman, preferably with children) in the khaki jungle uniform (always look for a police officer or someone whose uniform you recognize), and had been taken by a special electric car back to the main station at the far end of the park.

The young zookeeper in the information booth radioed ahead to the station that Ruby's parents had been found, and we trudged across the park. No electric car for us. We found our daughter enjoying a strawberry banana smoothie and regaling the other lost children with the tale of her pluck.

"Sweetie," I said, once we'd hugged her and reassured ourselves that she was fine. "Next time, before you go looking for the authorities, maybe you should make sure you're really lost. We were right there."

"But I didn't see you."

"I know, and you did the right thing, but next time just yell first, okay? Call for Mama or Daddy before you go off looking for someone else."

"There was no point in calling you," she said with great irritation. "If I called Mama then all the mothers would have just turned around. What would be the point of that?"

"Well," I said. "You can call 'Juliet' or you can trust me to recognize your voice."

She shook her head, disgusted at this. She adjusted the San Diego Zoo cap the counselor in the lost children's room had given her for comfort and consolation. Of the two of us, I was the one who needed consoling. Ruby seemed downright thrilled by her exploit. I, on the other hand, was ready to go home.

"I think we've all had enough animals for the day," I said.

Thirty

IN the car on the way back home to Los Angeles, I called Chantelle and Thomas's house. I reached only their machine.

When we pulled into our driveway I said to Peter, "You know, I think it's a safe bet that if Dr. Thomas Green is not at home, then he's at the hospital. If I tank the baby up would you mind if I go over to UCLA?"

Peter shook his head. "Sure, just nurse her as much as she'll take. If she needs more before bed I can defrost some milk. I know, I know. Don't put the bottles in the microwave."

* * *

DR. Thomas Green was on duty, but he was in surgery.

"Do you think he'll be a while?" I asked the nurse.

She looked at me over the tops of her half-glasses. She was a middle-aged African-American woman with pressed hair and a constellation of small moles, like freckles, scattered over her cheeks. "Are you a patient?" she said.

"No. It's personal."

She pursed her lips and blew air out through her nose with a disgusted huff. "I'm sure it is," she said. "He's doing a bowel resection, and he's been in there for over three hours. He'll be out soon. You can wait for him over there."

"Thank you," I said and did my best to give her a winning and grateful smile.

She shook her head in disgust. "Don't go bothering the patient's family."

I sat down, trying not to intrude on the waiting couple as they hovered nervously over their chairs, their eyes glued to the clock. About twenty minutes later, the doors at the end of the hall opened, and a man strode confidently through. He was strikingly handsome, with skin the deep brown of polished walnut, round eyes the size of quarters lushly fringed with lashes, a long straight nose, and a dimple in his chin. When they saw him, the couple leapt to their feet.

"The surgery went beautifully," he said. "Everything was better than we could have hoped for." He took the man's hand in his and shook it firmly, then he allowed the woman to embrace him.

"Dr. Green, we're so grateful for everything you've done

for Jonathan," the woman said. She wiped her streaming eyes. "You've been a blessing for him, and for us."

"It's that boy who's the blessing. The last thing he said before he went under was that he has finals at the end of the month and he's counting on us to get him well enough to take them on time."

The woman laughed and her husband clapped Chantelle's husband on the back a few times. Thomas wished them good-bye and turned to leave.

"Excuse me, Dr. Green," I said.

He turned back. "Yes?"

"I wonder if I could have a few minutes of your time. I'm Juliet Applebaum, the person Heavenly hired?" I didn't want to use the words private investigator in front of his patient's parents.

He wrinkled his brow for a moment and then said, "Yes, of course." He looked around the waiting room. "Why don't we go in here," he said, opening the double doors. "We'll have a little more privacy." He led me across a busy hall bustling with nurses to a small lounge. "How can I help you?" he said once we'd sat down.

"I just have a few questions."

"By all means."

"How well did you know Violetta?"

He settled back on a nubbly orange chair, crossing his long legs. "Chantelle and I have been together for nearly nine years, since our junior year of college. Back when we first met, Violetta was just a girl, fifteen years old. I met her when I went home with Chantelle to family dinners, that kind of thing. Honestly, she didn't make much of an impression. By the time Chantelle and I were seriously involved, Violetta was already gone most of the time. Then I heard about her more than I saw her, if you know what I mean. Corentine was beside herself, but it was clear from early on that the girl was a lost cause."

"Heavenly said there were periods when she would come home, periods when she tried to stop using drugs?"

He nodded, tenting his fingers in front of his chest. It leant him a professorial air. "She did try, especially when she was pregnant with Vashon. During that period we saw more of her. I was in medical school by then, so I didn't spend much time with the family, but Chantelle and I got married right before Vashon was born, and I know Violetta had hoped to be sober enough to come to the wedding."

"Hoped?"

He shook his head. "It was a great disappointment to Chantelle that her little sister wasn't there. My poor wife had two sisters, and neither of them was sufficiently sober to act as her bridesmaid. She ended up having two of her sorority sisters stand up with her."

Dr. Green's voice was deep and sweet, melodic even. I found myself wondering if I'd put on lipstick before I left the house, and if my hair was a wild mess from my day rushing around the zoo.

"Chantelle told me that you were the one who tracked Violetta down to let her know that Annette died."

He nodded. "The rest of the family was overwhelmed. Completely distraught. You have to understand that Annette's disease came as a complete surprise to them, to all of us. Had I known she was HIV positive, I would have arranged for her to receive treatment. The first any of us found out about it, the first *she* found out about it, was when she became ill with pneumonia. I imagine that she must have had symptoms before that, but she probably attributed them to . . . well, to hard living I suppose. At any rate, she died almost immediately."

"How did you find Violetta?"

"I looked where they told me to look, up and down Figueroa. It didn't take very long. I probably drove around for no more than half an hour before I saw her standing on a street corner."

"Was she surprised to see you?"

"I imagine. She was certainly disappointed when she realized I wasn't a potential client." He glanced at his watch.

"But she was willing to go with you?"

He arched one eyebrow. "Let's say she allowed herself to be convinced."

"Convinced?"

"I offered her a hundred dollars to get into the car, come to our house to get cleaned up, and attend her sister's funeral."

"You paid her to go to the funeral?"

"The family needed her to be there. Corentine and Chantelle needed her to be there. Had she been sober she would have realized that and come right away. But she was not. She was high on something, and she insisted I compensate her for her time. Which I did."

"Did anyone know you paid her to be there?"

He shook his head. "No. Of course not. It would have broken their hearts. Chantelle and Corentine were both so pleased to see her. Violetta had disappointed them so many times before, and I don't think they had high hopes. But when she came, it was like none of those previous disappointments had ever happened. Chantelle put her to bed in our guest room; she gave her clothes to wear to the wake the next day. She even bought her a dress for the funeral. My wife allowed herself to imagine that Violetta might be able to get clean, if she only had the help. She even managed to convince me that we should pay for her to go into rehab."

The way Chantelle had told the story, it was her husband's generosity that led to that offer.

"Did you think Violetta might actually go to rehab?"

He sighed. "Look, before the woman would get in my car, she took the hundred dollars I gave her, walked back to the corner, and scored herself some heroin. Of course I didn't think she'd get clean. That was Chantelle's dream, not mine, and certainly not Violetta's. The night after the funeral Chantelle found her sister shooting up in our bathroom."

"Chantelle said you threw her out."

A small smile played at the corner of his lips. "She said that? Well, I guess I did. My wife was screaming like an injured cat, dragging her sister by the hair and crying like . . . well, like she'd just buried one sister and found the other shooting dope, I suppose. I got between them and told Violetta to take her things and go."

"When did you see her again after that?"

"I suppose the next time was Vashon's birthday party. She was living at home, and she seemed actually to be doing okay. She'd been sober for two weeks. It was hard to believe she'd stay sober, and I know by that point Chantelle had lost faith in her. She didn't even allow herself to hope it would last. Poor Corentine got her heart broken all over again. She did every time that girl turned up. She's a good woman, Corentine, but her greatest flaw is her ability to be disappointed afresh by her children."

"The last time you saw Violetta, on the Sunday night before she died, she got drunk, didn't she?"

For the first time since I'd begun talking to him, Thomas looked uncomfortable. He shifted in his seat, uncrossing his legs and then recrossing them. "That was my fault, I suppose," he said finally. "It was my beer; I brought it to Corentine's. I shouldn't have let her have any, but giving in to Violetta was so much easier than fighting her." He smiled suddenly. "I guess you could say she had a lot in common with Chantelle in that way. The Spees women are all tenacious, stubborn women. Violetta just used her will to get herself high."

"And your wife? How does she use her will?"

He laughed. "To get me to do what she wants. What else?"

His laugh was a low-pitched rumble, deep and unabashedly sexy. Now it was my turn to shift uncomfortably in my seat.

I plowed on. "Ronnie and Heavenly both told me that

on occasion Violetta acted in inappropriate ways with them. Sexually inappropriate ways. Did she ever do anything like that with you?"

He made a disgusted face. "She knew better than to try. Even if she hadn't been a prostitute with heaven only knows what venereal diseases, I would never have tolerated it for a minute."

"But she never did try?"

He shrugged. "She flirted, I suppose. All you women flirt, don't you?"

I thought I was doing a pretty remarkable job of *not* flirting. "She never offered you sex or tried to touch you?"

"No," he said. "I suppose even Violetta knew better than to cross her sister like that. Besides, she knew she wasn't my type."

"What is your type?" I should have clamped my hands over my mouth before I let those words out.

He smiled and closed one eye in a slow, almost languid wink.

Thirty-one

ON my way out of the hospital I noticed the woman who had originally directed me to the waiting area. She was sitting at the nurses' station, talking to two other nurses. I walked over and stood there a moment until they noticed me.

"Yes, can I help you?" she asked, her tone as hostile as it had been when I first asked where I could find Chantelle's husband. "Did you take care of your 'personal business' with Dr. Green?" She used both her fingers and her voice to put the words "personal business" in quotation marks. One of the other nurses, a round Filipina woman with hair dyed a shade of red very close to my own, snickered. The other nurse rolled her eyes.

"I work for his sister-in-law," I said.

The first woman narrowed her eyes. "Do you?"

"Yes," I said. "Dr. Green was kind enough to help his sister-in-law and me out with some urgent family business."

She snorted. "Well, I don't doubt that. He's a 'kind' man." Again in quotation marks, although this time without the help of her fingers.

The third nurse, a petite African-American woman with close-cropped hair and a series of small hoop earrings running from her earlobes halfway up her ears, said, "She's not his type, anyway. She's probably already graduated from high school."

The other nurses laughed.

I leaned my elbows on the counter and said, "Does the handsome Dr. Green have a little problem with young girls?" I modulated my voice to match theirs, light and teasing, with more than a tang of bitterness.

The nurse with my red hair suddenly seemed to realize that they'd been talking out of school. "Oh no. He doesn't go with girls. Not like that. No little girls. Just . . ."

"Young women?"

"*Very* young women," the nurse with all the earrings said.

The nurse who had started this all in the first place said, "Enough. We're bad. We talk too much. Is there anything else you need?"

I rocked back on my heels. "Okay," I said. "Listen, I'm an investigator, and now you've given me the impression that Dr. Green is some kind of pedophile. So why don't you tell me exactly what's going on. Because I can't imagine you want me to go back to work thinking that, do you?"

They exchanged a glance and then the Filipina nurse said, "We're just teasing, you know? He never goes after real young girls. Just the medical students. To us they seem young, but they're not children. They're, what?" She turned to her coworkers. "They're like twenty-two, twenty-three years old, right?"

"At least," the first nurse said.

The nurse with the earrings motioned me closer. "Look, we didn't mean to get Dr. Green in trouble. He's not a pedophile. It's just that when a fine brother like him cheats on his wife, it bothers us. But don't get the wrong idea. He's not a criminal or anything. Those girls are all adults."

I lowered my voice. "I understand. Is he seeing anyone in particular?"

She shook her head. "Now, that's none of my business." It was a little late for that, and she had the grace to look embarrassed at her sudden discretion.

The first nurse said, "All we're saying is that every once in a while Dr. Green gets a thing going with one of the medical students. It's not so unusual, you know? It happens." She took the arm of the red-haired nurse and pulled her away. As they walked down the hall the first nurse shook her head and looked down at her computer screen, getting back to her work.

I turned to walk to the elevator bank but she called out, "Excuse me."

I looked back at her. "We were just talking," she said.

"We didn't mean anything by it." Her voice had completely lost its ring of bitter humor. She just sounded worried, and embarrassed that they had allowed themselves to be so indiscrete.

"Don't worry," I said. "It's all right."

But was it? I wondered. I had no idea whether he was just a flirt, or if he was actually involved with the young med students of whom the nurses were so suspicious. And more importantly, I had no idea what this meant for the purposes of my case.

I decided to call Heavenly. In the background I could hear music playing. "*Kind of Blue*?" I said.

"Yes," she said. "I always listen to Miles when I'm feeling low."

"You're feeling low tonight?" I hated the idea of bringing her even lower, but perhaps that was better than ruining a joyful mood.

"I was just thinking about my sisters, and my brothers, too. How hard things were for all of them, how hard my mother tried to save them."

"What do you think will happen when your brothers get out of prison?" I asked.

"I just don't know. They'll be older men by then, but it's hard for a black man with no education to get work even when he doesn't have a prison record. And with a record, who's going to hire them? Who's going to give them a chance?" She sighed, and then seemed to shake herself. "Anyway, that's not what you're calling me about. What's going on? Have you found out anything new?"

I paused, drumming my fingers on the steering wheel

for a moment. I was talking on my car speakerphone while I drove home. "No," I said finally. "Not really. I just have a question for you. Do you think it's at all possible that your brother-in-law and Violetta might have been having an affair? Or that something might have been going on between them?"

She gave a bark of horrified laughter. "Thomas? You've got to be kidding me, girl. Have you *met* Thomas?"

"I met him tonight. I paid a visit to the hospital."

"So you know that my brother-in-law is a very handsome man. He's a doctor. He doesn't have much money now, but he will have plenty when he finishes his residency. The last person in world he would look at would be someone like Violetta. And he loves Chantelle. They've been together for something like ten years. He'd never do something like that."

"Not even in a moment of weakness? If Violetta made a play for him, like what she did to you?"

"No. Never. His reaction would be the same as mine was. He'd have thrown her out on her narrow behind."

I mulled this over for a moment as I turned into the street that wound up through the canyon to my house. When I'd asked Thomas himself, he had expressed profound disgust at the idea, and he neither seemed to be protesting too much nor covering up anything. Still, Heavenly's argument about his love for Chantelle seemed to mean little given what I'd heard from the nurses.

"Heavenly," I said. "I found out something tonight about Thomas. I feel awful telling you this, and I certainly don't want you to tell Chantelle, but the nurses at the hospital where Thomas works told me he has a reputation for . . . well . . . getting involved with medical students. It's certainly possible that they were just passing along false rumors, but I wonder if that changes your mind about the possibility of something having happened between him and Violetta."

She sighed. "Women do not understand this kind of thing. Honestly, sometimes I'm glad I was born a man. It gives me perspective that the rest of you just do not have. I never said I don't think Thomas fools around. Hell, he's a *man*. Men are dogs, don't you know that yet? And he's a good-looking man. Of course he fools around. That's what men do. What I'm saying is that he wouldn't fool around with *Violetta*. I loved my sister, but I know what she was. She was a drug-addicted prostitute. She was a crack ho. Thomas would never have touched her, if for no other reason than because he would have been afraid of catching something from her. And Thomas loves Chantelle. He wouldn't hurt her by being with her sister. Now, is that love going to last forever? I don't know. You can never know. I was the first one to tell my sister that she should get something in writing before she went and put that man through medical school, because I know men. I know that just because he loves you now doesn't mean that ten years from now, he won't trade you in for a newer, younger model. But whatever Thomas is doing or not doing, I can tell you for sure, he never did anything with Violetta."

By now I had arrived home and was parked in my driveway. "Okay, I'm sure you're right," I said. "Heavenly, we're getting close to the time when we have to concede defeat. I'm not sure there's much more I can do and I don't want to waste any more of your money. The answer to who killed Violetta most likely lies in a some trick she picked up that night. If that's the case, then the kind of search that could lead to the discovery of the murderer is something I don't have the resources to accomplish. I can try to encourage the police to do a dragnet, I can try to encourage them to at the very least put an officer out there for a few weeks to run every license plate looking for men with histories of violence, but frankly, I don't have a lot of faith that the cops will agree to do it or that even if they did they would come up with anything. That's why I haven't tried to do that kind of thing myself. It's like searching for the proverbial needle in the haystack. It's been six months. The chances of that man coming back again, the chances of them spotting him, the chances that there will be any evidence, are not high. We have the DNA, but it's possible that came from someone else entirely."

Heavenly's voice was thick with tears. She suddenly sounded a lot more like what she must have before her sex change. "So now what?"

I sat silently, considering her question. "Let's sleep on things and talk again tomorrow," I said.

After she hung up the phone I still didn't get out of the car. I sat there in the dark, thinking about my failure. I tried to remind myself that I had accomplished something tremendously important in this case, perhaps the most important thing I'd achieved in my entire career. I'd forced the police to revisit an entire group of cases, and that had resulted in the arrest of a man who would have gone on killing for a very long time. I'd been part of saving the lives of any number of women. Shouldn't my failure to find Violetta's murderer pale in comparison to that?

I restarted the engine, and pulled the car out of the driveway. I had to give it one more shot. Just one. Then I would let it go.

Thirty-two

My cell phone rang almost immediately. "Where are you going?" Peter said. "I heard your car in the driveway, and then you pulled out again. What's going on?"

"I'm going to Figueroa Street."

"Goddamnit, Juliet. You promised you wouldn't go back there."

"I'm not going anywhere near Sylvester, I promise. I'm just going to the taco truck. This is the last time, I promise. I have to, Peter. Before I quit this case I have to be sure that I've done everything I can."

Peter knows me like no one else does. He can hear the slightest change in the timbre of my voice; he knows what I'm feeling, sometimes before I do.

"Stay in the car, okay?" he said. "Don't get out. Just

pull in the parking lot, and ask whoever you want to talk to to get in the car with you. And if you see that Sylvester guy, swear to me that you'll book the hell out of there as fast as you can."

"I promise," I said.

"And keep your phone on. I'm going to sit on the line with you."

"That's crazy, Peter."

"I don't care if it's crazy. It'll make me feel better."

"Okay."

When I got to the taco truck I said, "I'm going to turn the volume down so they won't be able to hear the static and realize that the phone is on. Just don't talk, okay?"

"Fine."

I pulled into the parking lot and up next to the truck. Baby Richard was in his usual spot on the bench. As I rolled down my window I saw Jackie getting out of a car that had just pulled up to the curb in front of Baby Richard. She blew a kiss to the driver of the car and handed her nephew something. M&M was sitting next to Baby Richard.

"Hey, Mary Margaret," I called.

She looked up from the donut she was eating. She seemed neither pleased nor displeased to see me.

"Want to get warm?" I said. It was a cool night, an edge of damp in the air. The morning fog was rolling in early.

She glanced over at Baby Richard. He shrugged. "Okay," she said. She hopped up into the passenger seat and wrinkled her nose. What did it mean when a Figueroa Street prostitute was disturbed by the odor in my minivan?

"One of my kids got sick in the backseat yesterday," I said.

"My daughter gets real carsick," she said. "She's got to ride in the front or else she just pukes her guts up."

I decided that a lecture on the danger of allowing a small child to ride in the front seat would be lost on her.

"Hey!" Jackie called, knocking on my window. "Open the door."

I pushed the automatic door button and it glided open.

"Oh my goodness," she said. "I seen that on TV." She got in the car and scraped the food wrappings, stuffed animals and Uno cards from the seat onto the floor. "Close that door now, I'm freezing. Juliet, you owe me a buck twenty five."

"What? Why?"

She held up her coffee cup. I laughed and pulled two dollars out of the armrest where I kept my change and small bills. "Here," I said. "Now you owe me. You want me to pay for yours, M&M?"

M&M shook her head. "S'okay. Baby Richard bought it for me."

"Whew," Jackie said. "Like my ol' auntie Florene used to say, it smells like a sack o' granddaddies in here."

"Sorry," I said. "Isaac gets carsick."

"So," Jackie said. "What you doing down here again? You looking for Sylvester, maybe beat his sorry ass?" She cackled. Clearly Baby Richard's sense of humor was an inherited trait.

"No," I said. "I'm just tying up some loose ends on Violetta's case. I wanted to make sure there was nothing else you remembered from the night she was killed. Can you think of anything? Anything at all?"

M&M shook her head. "It was just a regular night, you know?"

"And you're sure you can't remember who picked her up?"

She shook her head. "She had a couple of dates early in the night, and then we got some coffee over here and went back out on the corner. We stood out for a while, and then I had a date. She was gone when I got back."

"And you, Jackie? Do you remember seeing anything?"

Jackie blew on her coffee and shook her head. "It was just a night, you know? Like every night. I don't even remember seeing her much. Next thing I heard she was dead."

"Did you guys know Annette?"

"Sure we did," Jackie said. "Sure we did, Lord rest her soul. I got an AIDS test after she died. Just to be sure, you know? It was negative. I'm clean as they come. But I never touch needles. Annette, she used needles all the time."

"What about you, M&M?" I asked.

"I knew her," she said. "She was real sweet. She used to help me and Violetta out at the beginning. You know, show us stuff. Like Jackie does."

Jackie smiled proudly. "I'm a real mother hen to the young girls. Teach them how to get what's they due. All that."

"Do you remember when Annette died? Violetta's brother-in-law came to get her for the funeral. Did either of you see him?"

Jackie hooted. "Sure I did. Mm-mm." She licked her lips.

"I didn't see him," M&M said. "But I know he was real generous with Violetta. He gave her money sometimes, and didn't ask nothing about what she was going to use it for."

"When did he give her money? When Annette died?"

M&M shrugged. "Yeah, then again a couple of days before Violetta died. He came down here like he did that other time when Annette died, but this time he didn't take Violetta away with him. She just sat in his car with him for a little while, and when she came out she told me he gave her a lot of money."

"How much?" I felt a rising excitement.

Jackie said, "Enough that she bought five hundred dollars worth of dope from Baby Richard. And not junk, either. The really nice stuff. The kind he keeps for hisself. She was flying on that dope until the night she died."

"She didn't just buy dope with it," M&M said. "Violetta gave me back two hundred dollars she owed me, and she was planning on buying her son a Game Boy. She was going to give it to him the next time she saw him. She was going to buy her mama some real nice new shoes. Her mama wears these special shoes, because her feet are like fat, but small. Like a weird size, and they hurt her real bad. I heard Violetta tell her mama that she was going to buy her a new pair of shoes."

"When was that?"

M&M shrugged. "I don't know, I guess the day after she got the money? The day before she died, I think."

"Mary Margaret, did Violetta tell you why Thomas gave her the money?"

She shook her head. "She just said he was trying to play her, but he was messing with the wrong girl. That's all she said."

"And you don't know how much money?"

"Sylvester knows," Jackie said. "She was waving it around so much, he found out she had it and took it away from her."

"All of it?"

"Oh, he probably left her a little, you know. Just to keep her from going crazy," Jackie said.

I looked at M&M. "Do you know what happened with the money?"

She nodded. "He took it. But he said he'd buy her some new clothes with it, so she should be quiet. She was real upset, though. She cried hard."

"When was that?"

"The day before she died. She didn't even want to work that night, she was so upset. But Sylvester made her. It was lucky she bought all that stuff off of Baby Richard, because Sylvester never found it, and it made her feel a lot better."

"Hey," Jackie said. "You gonna buy us some more coffee?"

"Jackie," I replied, "I'm going to buy you anything you want."

Thirty-three

THE next morning I drove right from dropping the older kids off to Corentine's house. She answered the door wearing a pale pink robe and a pair of quilted slippers at least two sizes too large for her feet. When she saw me, her hands lifted to her hair. It was wrapped tightly around her head in a dark brown nylon scarf.

"Oh my," she said. "I'm not even dressed."

"I'm sorry, Corentine. But I have to talk to you. Can I come in?"

"What a pretty little baby," she said. She didn't open the door.

"Please, Corentine."

She looked back over her shoulder into the house. "I

don't usually like to have visitors before I get the house fixed up a bit."

"Please," I said.

She sighed. "Just understand that I haven't done my housework yet. I was going to get to it right now."

The house was no messier than any house with children on a school-day morning—laundry spilled out of a plastic basket in the front hall, shoes tumbled haphazardly in the middle of the floor, and the remains of breakfast on the kitchen table. It looked, in fact, a lot better than the house I'd left behind me that morning. I put Sadie down in the living room. She had fallen asleep in her car seat and I didn't want her to wake up. Corentine began clearing dishes and putting away the milk and the boxes of cereal.

"I usually cook a hot meal for breakfast," she said. "I don't like to let them go out with just cereal in their stomachs, but I been a little tired."

"You should see what my kids eat. Half the time I can't even get them to eat a bowl of cereal."

"Oh, you've got to make them sit until they eat. They can't concentrate in school if they don't have a nice breakfast warming them up. I tell that to mine all the time. It's just too hard to pay attention to the teacher with your stomach rumbling, and lunchtime is a long time away."

She turned on the water and began scrubbing the dishes. I took up a dishtowel and started drying. She smiled at me. "I'm not even going to tell you that you don't need to do that," she said, "because I know you will no matter what I say."

"Corentine," I said as I wiped the plastic cereal bowls dry. "Did you talk to Violetta before she died? After that Sunday dinner when you had to ask her to leave?"

Corentine sighed heavily and wiped her forehead with the back of one soapy hand. She left a spot of foam on her forehead and I leaned over and blotted it gently with the towel.

"Thank you, honey," she said. "Lord this house is a mess." She stood with her hands in the warm soapy water, not washing the dishes, just holding them still under the bubbles.

"Here, let me," I said. I put my hands in the water next to hers and gently but quickly washed the remaining dishes. Then I drained the water out of the sink. She held her hands out obediently as I rinsed them and my own.

She allowed me to lead her to the table and sat down. I poured her a cup of coffee and she sat, her hands cupped around the mug. I made short work of the countertops. I found a broom behind the door and swept the floor. I glanced over my shoulder to see if she would protest as I went into the living room to clean up the children's toys and shoes, but she didn't, just stared into the cooling coffee in her cup. After the living room was in order I quickly made the beds, smoothing the covers and doing my best at hospital corners. Within twenty minutes I'd done more house cleaning in Corentine's apartment than I'd done in my own house since my kids were born.

I dumped out Corentine's now-cold coffee and poured her a fresh cup.

"Oh my," she said. "Oh my. I just sat here and let you

clean my house?" She sounded befuddled and dismayed.

"Corentine," I said. "Did you talk to your daughter before she died?"

She sighed and lifted the cup to her lips. Her teeth clacked against the rim and she set it down again. "Yes," she said, finally. "Yes, I talked to my baby."

"What happened?" I asked gently.

"It was bad."

"You can tell me."

"I didn't help her."

"You tried. I know you tried. You spent your whole life trying to help your daughter."

"Not that time."

"Please, Corentine. Please tell me what happened."

She sighed heavily. She tried again to drink from her mug, and this time succeeded in taking a tremulous sip. "It was the day before she died. She called about this time of day, maybe a little later. I know it was still morning, because I wasn't done getting the house to rights. Violetta wanted to talk to Vashon, but of course he was at school. I said, 'Girl, it's a school day. Your baby's in math class right now.' But I don't think she even knew the time of day. She kept talking about how she going to get him a Game Boy. She going to buy me a new pair of my orthopedic shoes. Talking such foolishness. Those shoes cost one hundred and twenty dollars. When did Violetta ever have that kind of money? For a little while I just let her go on and on, making those promises. I remember I was sweeping the floor, and I just put the phone on speaker and let her talk about that Game Boy and my shoes. And all sorts a other things she was going to buy Vashon and me. When I was done sweeping, that's when I did it." Corentine bit her lip.

"What? What did you do?"

She shrugged her heavy, rounded shoulders. "I told her she couldn't call me no more. I never said that to her before." She rubbed her eyes. "Oh dear Lord."

"She was high, wasn't she? You didn't want her calling like that."

She nodded. "I told her she couldn't call or come by no more. I told her that if she wanted to see her baby again she'd have to go into a real program. Lord help me, I told my poor girl that what she did to Ronnie was so evil, I wouldn't even let her talk to Vashon no more unless she got herself into a program." Corentine's mouth twisted miserably.

"I think you did the right thing," I said. "I mean, I know it probably doesn't mean much; why should you care what I think? But I've spent a long time representing drug users in court, and I can tell you that you don't do them any favors by making it easy for them to take advantage of you. You made it clear to your daughter that you would be there for her if she ever wanted to stop using. You told her you'd help her if she got into a program. That's more than a lot of people would have done considering all she'd put you through."

"I let her down."

"No, you didn't."

"I didn't help her."

"She didn't want to be helped."

"But she did! She did want to be helped. She called me again, the next day, the day she died, saying she didn't want to be out on the street no more and could she come home. I was stone cold. I told her that I meant what I said. I said she couldn't cross my threshold until after she'd been through rehab. I said I didn't believe her. And I told her what she did to her little brother made me sick." Corentine sobbed suddenly and put her face in her hands.

"Ronnie told me that after you talked to her she called him to apologize."

Corentine nodded, her face still hidden.

"Corentine, please. Please help me figure out what happened that night. Violetta called Ronnie to apologize, and then what happened?"

She raised her face. "The last words my baby girl heard from my mouth were angry words. Hateful words. Do you know what that feels like? She thought I didn't love her no more. She thought she couldn't come home no more. She died thinking her own mama didn't love her."

"That's not true."

"It is! It is true. She never knew that Ronnie called and told me about her apology. She never knew that I called up Chantelle and said that I was going to let her come home and that Thomas would need to find some real good program for her."

"You called Chantelle?"

"Yes."

"To tell her what exactly?"

"What I told you. That Violetta was finally serious

about the rehab, and that Thomas should find her a good place."

"What did Chantelle say?"

"Oh, you know. She was worried that Violetta wouldn't really do it, that she was just making promises. You got to understand, my girls used to be real close. They were closer even than twins. Chantelle just loved her sister. And Violetta, she broke Chantelle's heart over and over again. Chantelle tried to argue with me, but I said 'Look, we got to give Violetta another chance. Family is family and I only got two daughters left now.' Well, three, with Heavenly, but you know what I mean."

"And did she agree?"

"Of course she did. Thomas is a good man, and he promised once before to pay for Violetta to go into rehab."

"Did you try to call Violetta? Did you try to tell her that she could come home?"

Corentine started to cry, her tears running down the swells of her smooth, round cheeks. "I left her a message. The day she died I left her a message on her voice mail. I said, 'Violetta, baby, come on home.' I left her a message," she wept. "And I don't know, I don't know if she got it. I don't know if she died knowing she was welcome in my house."

"I'm sure she did," I said. "I'm sure she knew that. She always knew that."

Thirty-four

I wanted to see Chantelle and Thomas together, because I wanted to put him on the spot, to see if he was as smooth and unflappable in front of his wife as he was when she wasn't there. I called the cell phone number Heavenly gave me for Chantelle when the case first began.

"My shift ends at two," she said. "You can come over after that. Thomas will be home. It's his day off."

Having dumped Sadie on a grumbling Peter, I had no children with me when I walked up the steps to Chantelle and Thomas's impeccable house. Their front door was flanked by tubs of pink geraniums and the tiny front garden was a patch of bright green grass surrounded on all four sides by a row of miniature rosebushes, also pink.

Chantelle answered the door, still wearing her pink flowered scrubs. She clearly liked the color.

"Come in," she said.

The living room into which she led me had a cream-colored leather sectional sofa, silk flowers in cut glass vases on the end tables, and a fifty-inch flat-screen television dominating one wall. Chantelle left me alone on the couch and disappeared into the kitchen. It was clear that I was not meant to follow. A moment later she came out holding a tray with a coffeepot and a matching sugar bowl and creamer. She poured me a cup of coffee. She offered a plate of butter cookies, but I declined. She did not pour coffee for herself or for Thomas, who arrived a moment later, wearing jeans and a UCLA sweatshirt. His feet were bare, and I caught Chantelle giving them a disapproving glance.

"I just had a few things I wanted to verify," I said.

They looked at each other, and then at me.

I continued. "Before Violetta was killed, someone gave her a large sum of money. Probably over a thousand dollars. Do either of you know anything about that?"

Neither of them looked surprised, but neither answered me.

I waited.

After a few moments I said, "Look, Thomas, I know you gave her the money. There were witnesses." I didn't elaborate that those witnesses were drug-addled prostitutes who would have exactly zero credibility in a court of law. *I* believed Jackie and M&M, and I was betting that their existence would at least be enough to convince Thomas to tell me the truth.

It was a good bet.

"Twenty-five hundred," Thomas said. "It was twenty-five hundred dollars, not a thousand. We gave it to her. We gave it to her in return for promising to disappear, to leave her mother and the rest of the family alone once and for all."

Chantelle was breathing quickly. A thin sheen of sweat stood out on her forehead. "You need to understand," she said. "My sister Violetta did so much damage in her life. She hurt my mother over and over again. She hurt all of us. She was supposed to be my bridesmaid and she was too high to come to my wedding. And that wasn't even the worst thing she did. She made advances to my little brother. She was an evil, evil person."

I looked at Thomas, who shifted uncomfortably in his seat. Clearly, Chantelle didn't know that he'd had to bribe Violetta with heroin money to get her to come home for her sister Annette's funeral. If Chantelle had known about that she surely would have added it to the litany of Violetta's crimes against the family.

Chantelle's words tumbled out of her mouth. "She shot up here, in my house. She tortured that poor son of hers, showing up every couple of months and pretending she was ready to act like a mother to him. And Mama. She broke Mama's heart over and over again. Every time she promised to get clean and then ended up back on the street, Mama would just die inside a little more. My mother has diabetes, did you know that? And high blood pressure. The cycle of hope and disappointment was killing her. I just knew if I didn't do something Violetta was going to break Mama's heart for good and for real. I couldn't let that happen."

"So you paid her to go away."

Thomas said, "After that awful scene where she got drunk and behaved so appallingly—in front of her son, I might add—Chantelle and I decided that enough was enough. I emptied our bank account and I went down to Violetta's corner. I told her she could have it all, every last dime, as long as she promised never to show her face at home again. I told her she couldn't call or write. She had to disappear."

I looked from one of them to the other. Thomas sat easily in his chair, one arm thrown over the back, his long legs extended out before him and his bare feet crossed. Chantelle, however, was sitting on the edge of her matching armchair, her hands clasped, her face damp with sweat.

"But Violetta didn't go away, did she?"

Thomas shook his head. "I guess she didn't. Or she didn't plan to." He shrugged his shoulders ruefully. "Why we ever thought we could trust a drug addict's word, I'll never know. At her funeral we found out that the very next day—a day after taking every dime her sister and I had managed to save—she called up offering presents and asking to come home."

I frowned. "At her funeral?"

He nodded. "I'm surprised my mother-in-law survived

the funeral, if you want to know the truth. She was weeping over the casket, holding on to it like . . . like . . . well, like her child was inside. She was begging Violetta's forgiveness for not letting her come home like she'd asked. It just about broke my heart to see that. It broke all our hearts. Everyone in that room."

I stared at him. His face was wide open; sad and sorry. It's so hard to tell if someone is lying. Was he telling the truth or was he just very smooth? Chantelle, however, was much easier to read. She sat knotting her fingers in her lap, her head tucked to her chest, her lips pinched into a tight line and her eyes nearly closed. Beads of sweat had sprung out on her hairline.

"Chantelle," I said. "You knew about the call."

She shook her head violently from side to side.

"You did. Corentine called you. She told you that she thought Violetta was serious now and that Thomas should find her a good, private rehab center. She told you she wanted you to pay for it."

Chantelle shook her head again.

Thomas wrinkled his brow. "I think you must have your chronology confused. The first we heard about all that was after Violetta died."

"Chantelle?" I said.

"I don't remember," she whispered. "I don't remember."

"Chantelle? Baby?" Thomas said. "What's she talking about?"

I said, "Corentine told me she spoke to Chantelle, that she told her that Violetta had called and said she wanted to come home and try to get into rehab again. Corentine said she told Chantelle that this time she wanted Violetta to go into a better program, a private program, and that you would pay for it."

"That's not what happened," he said firmly. "Corentine must be remembering wrong. Or you must have misunderstood."

"Chantelle?" I said softly.

"Mama must be remembering wrong," she said. She unknotted her hands and wiped the palms on her knees. "Or you must have misunderstood."

"Thomas, do you mind telling me where you were the night Violetta was killed?" I said.

"Do I mind? Yes, I mind," he said, his angry voice suddenly booming through the room. "Who the hell do you think you are to be asking me that kind of question?"

"He was working," Chantelle said. "He was in surgery."

"Were you?"

"That is no business of yours," he said.

"Were you working, Thomas?" I repeated.

"I don't owe you an explanation, but I have nothing to hide. I was on call the night Violetta was killed. I remember quite clearly. I had back-to-back appendectomies. I have a hospital full of witnesses who can attest to my whereabouts."

Could he have had time to sneak out from the hospital and make it all the way to Figueroa Street? It seemed virtually impossible. What if someone went looking for him and he was nowhere to be found?

I looked at Chantelle. She was a tall woman, with large hands. Strong, capable, nurse's hands.

"Where were you, Chantelle?" I said in a gentle voice. "Where were you on the night Violetta was killed?"

"I was working," she said.

Thomas looked confused; his brows knitted together and his mouth open as if he were about to speak.

Chantelle repeated, "I was working."

Thomas stared at his wife. "Be quiet, baby," he said to her. "Don't say anything else." He stood up and pointed at me. "You, get out of this house. Get out right now." He put his body between Chantelle's and mine. "Go!" he shouted.

I left.

Thirty-five

I wrote my report for Heavenly that evening. It took a long time, and multiple drafts. My first version included what I saw when I looked at Chantelle's face as she created an alibi that her husband clearly knew was false. It included how I imagined the events took place. Chantelle received yet another phone call from her mother, the twentieth or thirtieth or two-hundreth saying that Violetta was coming home, that Violetta was going to try again, that Violetta was sure, this time, that she'd succeed in drying out. In Corentine's voice was all the hope of a desperate mother, the hope that Chantelle knew was doomed to be crushed. I will never know, but I don't think Chantelle drove down to Figureroa Street planning on hurting her sister. Perhaps she meant to plead with her to get out of town, perhaps all she wanted was her money back. In that first draft I put my own opinion, one that a defense expert could surely be found to validate, that the single blow to the back of her head had somehow been accidentally administered. Perhaps Chantelle had pushed Violetta, and she'd fallen and hit her head on the corner of the Dumpster behind which she was found. Perhaps Chantelle did hit her, but in a moment of rage, never intending to kill her. Or perhaps I am wrong, and Chantelle intended to kill her sister and leave her body in an alley near the corner where Violetta spent her life hustling money to feed her voracious habit.

That was not the draft I finally submitted to my client. What I gave Heavenly was more precise, more accurate. It included only what I knew for sure to be true, that Thomas had given Violetta money, twenty-five hundred dollars, and told her to go away. That Violetta had instead called her mother, offered gifts, and then, when the money was stolen by her pimp, asked to come home one more time. The report I submitted included Thomas's alibi, and Chantelle's claim of one. I wrote that these alibis could be easily verified.

With the report I included no bill. We would keep the small retainer Heavenly had given, I decided, but would accept no more. I did not expect to be paid for destroying a family.

I delivered the report to Heavenly the next day. Al insisted on accompanying me, and we arrived at her apartment in West Hollywood at seven o'clock in the morning. She answered the door wearing a silk blouse and skirt, her hair tucked into a hairnet. I'd never seen her without her wig before.

Wordlessly I handed her the report while Al stood, his arms crossed in front of his chest, looking stern but uncomfortable.

We stood in the doorway while Heavenly tore open the envelope and skimmed through the document.

"What does this mean?" she said. "Are you trying to tell me that they might not have been working that night? What difference does that make? So she and Thomas gave Violetta money? So what? We all gave Violetta money."

"There is no physical evidence in the case. There was no one who saw anything, there are no fingerprints, there is no weapon. All there is, is the money," I said. "You hired me to find out what happened to your sister, and I've done the best I can."

We left Heavenly standing in her doorway, the pages crumpled between her long and impeccably manicured fingers.

It took me a long time to decide if it was the right thing to do, but finally I called Detective Jarin. He never returned my calls, so eventually I wrote him a short note. I wrote about the money Thomas and Chantelle had given Violetta before she died. I wrote about the promise Violetta had made in taking it, and about how she broke that promise. Those were the facts I had discovered. Creating a narrative to explain those facts was up to him. In the end, he did what I had expected him to do: nothing. Perhaps he interviewed Thomas and Chantelle, perhaps he didn't even bother to do that. I'll never know. There were no arrests made in the case.

I've done my best to keep up with the women on Figueroa Street. I visit from time to time. I buy a round of hot coffee. Sometimes I eat a burrito with Baby Richard. Jackie's still out there, hustling. She's a grandmother now, but that doesn't seem to cramp her style. M&M left town a few months after I finished my investigation. She told me she was going to try her luck in Shreveport, that she had an aunt there who said she could stay with her until she got on her feet. She was talking about going to beauty school and learning how to do hair extensions. I don't know if there's much call in Louisiana for a white girl with that particular expertise, but I gave M&M some money and my phone number. She surely spent the former, but hasn't made any use of the latter.

I heard once more from Heavenly. I guess she knew somehow that I'd want to keep up a little, especially with her mother. Heavenly sent me a Christmas card that included one of those Christmas letters. Corentine's heart surgery had gone very well, the letter said. She'd had an angioplasty and was doing better than anyone could have hoped. The letter also let me and its presumably multitude of other recipients know that since things were a little hard for Corentine right now the children were staying with their aunts. Chantelle had the girls. And Vashon? Vashon was with Heavenly. And he was doing just great. Enrolled in private school. On the soccer team. Got his wish of an iPod for Christmas. And Heavenly was doing her best to shake up his new school's parents association. By all accounts they were both blossoming.

I don't know what narrative Heavenly, Chantelle, and Thomas have created to explain the facts I discovered, or whether their various narratives have any bearing on the truth. I do know this: In a while the murder of Violetta Spees will be transferred to the cold case unit, perhaps to the desk of Detective Stephen Sherman. At that time he'll see the note I wrote, and perhaps he will make up a narrative of his own.

"A master of smart, snappy repartee."
—*Kirkus Reviews*

Praise for
THE CRADLE ROBBERS

"Customary humor . . . dependably tart mommy-track wisecracks."
—*Kirkus Reviews*

"Witty . . . smart sleuthing." —*The New York Times Book Review*

"Human and credible characters—in particular, a smart, sensitive sleuth . . . should delight committed fans and attract new ones."
—*Publishers Weekly*

"Fabulous." —*Midwest Book Review*

"Waldman always provides full-bodied characters, humor, and a socially conscious plot that entertains as it enlightens."
—*Booklist*

MURDER PLAYS HOUSE

"Well-plotted . . . Juliet is a wonderful invention, warm, loving, and sympathetic to those in need, but unintimidated by the L.A. entertainment industry she must enter to search for clues . . . What a motive, what a resolution, and how clever of Juliet to figure it out."
—*Publishers Weekly*

"The Mommy-Track Mysteries get progressively feistier and wittier."
—*Midwest Book Review*

"As always, Waldman uses humor to portray the Los Angeles scene while making some serious points about what is really important in life. This thoroughly modern cozy will be popular."
—*Booklist*

"Witty Waldman is so endearingly pro-kid that you may run right out and get pregnant, and so unsparing about Hollywood sylphs and pro-anorexia websites that you may never diet again."
Kirkus Reviews

continued . . .

DEATH GETS A TIME-OUT

"Juliet and her patient husband make an appealing couple—funny, clever, and loving (but never mawkish). Waldman has an excellent ear for the snappy comeback, especially when delivered by a five-year-old." —*Publishers Weekly*

"Waldman is at her witty best when dealing with children, carpooling, and first-trimester woes, but is no slouch at explaining the pitfalls of False Memory Syndrome either."

—*Kirkus Reviews*

"Think *Chinatown*, but with strollers and morning sickness. Arguably the best of Waldman's mysteries."

—*Long Island Press*

A PLAYDATE WITH DEATH

"Smoothly paced and smartly told."

—*The New York Times Book Review*

"Sparkling . . . Witty and well-constructed . . . Those with a taste for lighter mystery fare are sure to relish the adventures of this contemporary, married, mother-of-two Nancy Drew."

—*Publishers Weekly*

"[A] deft portrayal of Los Angeles's upper crust and of the dilemma facing women who want it all." —*Booklist*